CHARLIE'S WORLD

OF

GLITTERING POWERS

TRACY RAWLES

Matador
9 Priory Business Park,
Wistow Road, Kibworth Beauchamp,
Leicestershire. LE8 0RX
Tel: 0116 279 2299
Email: books@troubador.co.uk
Web: www.troubador.co.uk/matador
Twitter: @matadorbooks

ISBN 978 1784624 736

British Library Cataloguing in Publication Data.
A catalogue record for this book is available from the British Library.

Printed and bound in the UK by TJ International, Padstow, Cornwall
Typeset in 11.5pt Aldine by Troubador Publishing Ltd, Leicester, UK

Matador is an imprint of Troubador Publishing Ltd

*With love to Mum and Dad, who are always in my pocket!
To Jonathan and Karen, love always. Thank you all for the
many cherished memories, which made this story possible.*

ACKNOWLEDGEMENTS

With sincere thanks to everyone at Troubador Publishing Ltd (Matador) for making the publishing process so seamless.

I give heartfelt thanks to Leo Hartas for his wonderful illustration.

Last but not least, thanks to the Cornish Pasty Association. I look forward to eating my next traditional Cornish pasty!

CHARLIE'S WORLD OF GLITTERING POWERS

CHAPTER 1

THE OLD WINEGROWER
AND THE CHARCOAL CIGALE

It was as dark as pitch. With just a small lantern to light up the inside of the stone military pillbox, the old winegrower stirred into an open-topped oak barrel grape juice and the dye from the petals of Provençal wildflowers. Before he added a sprinkling of his secret ingredient, he pulled a small book, sealed with mystical cigale and forest folklore charms, from his jacket pocket, which he then placed inside the barrel of sparkling bubbles.

The old man smiled happily, bowed his head and wiped his brow with the back of a weather-beaten hand. He stooped as he poked his head through the doorway; there was one last gust from the Mistral wind and the forest became calm.

In the barrel, the mix splattered and popped sending spirals of glitter towards the pitted roof of the old, grey building. Owls screeched overhead as the winegrower pushed the six-wheeled oak barrel, with its sparkling, enchanted mix, onto the limestone pathway. Coils of apple wood smoke from the winegrower's house

danced along the valley of vines and pines, circling both the barrel and the pillbox.

Whoosh! The mix with its violet, purple and gold sparks soared high above the pine tree forest, streaming glittering flakes up towards the stars. The cigale folklore charms released a beam of golden light that shone brightly against the sapphire blue sky. The book spun in the air and with one final swirl drifted downwards, where it landed close to a stack of pinecones at the entrance to the pillbox.

With a dazzling explosion of colour, the sparkling glitter tumbled like a horsetail firework through lofty, green-leafed pine trees, casting its mystical, violet-coloured dye over the cover of the winegrower's pocket-sized book.

Years later in a Cornish stone cottage, twinkling fairy lights that decorated the conservatory windows sparkled like a star on a Christmas tree. December 25th had long been and gone, but the brightly shining lights remained in place. The fairy lights not only lit the conservatory with a warm glow, but also shone across the hallway into the reading room with its aged buckled walls and polished wooden floors.

A pair of brown eyes raced along the rows of books that filled eight wooden shelves. The shelves were set inside a deep alcove with the eighth shelf almost touching the sloping, beamed ceiling. There was so much choice, but which one? Sevi's eyes suddenly stopped skating over the rows of hardbacks and paperbacks when they fell upon a small pocket-sized

book with a violet cover. As she looked closely at its spine of purple letters, it appeared to jiggle and wiggle before her eyes. 'Whoa,' she said, stepping forward to take a closer look.

Sevi blinked hard and then reaching out she pulled the book towards her. Her tummy fluttered with excitement just as it would have done had it been Christmas Eve.

The sparkling purple letters on the narrow spine spelt the words – *The Mix for Provençal Snuffle-Buzzers*.

'Umm, what is this all about? I don't know what Provençal Snuffle-Buzzers are, but I do know we are going to Provence on holiday. This could be a good book to take with me,' Sevi said.

In an armchair next to the bookshelves, Sevi sat quietly holding the book under the light of a table lamp. Eagerly she flicked open the glittering pages, but to her disappointment each page was full of codes, symbols and what looked like a foreign language. Frustrated, she held the book so tightly her knuckles turned white. 'Oh my days! I'm going boss-eyed,' whispered Sevi. 'I know a little French, but this is not French. All these weird codes and words I do not understand. How annoying.'

Page after page of glittering, golden coded letters twinkled before her eyes. She curled further into the soft, springy armchair and tried to decode the letters and symbols. Sevi was completely bewildered yet fascinated by the wonders of the violet book. 'What does it all mean and how long have we had this book?' Sevi asked herself. 'I've never noticed it before.'

Evening had turned to night. Feeling tired Sevi closed the book and looked at the violet cover. Drawn in charcoal was a sketch of a winged bug on a pine tree. Brushing her fingers gently over the bug she thought for a moment that its wings flickered, releasing a dash of glitter. 'Whoa, glitter! What's going on?'

Sevi's eyes widened. 'That's weird. I only touched the drawing for a split second, where's the bug gone?' All that remained on the front cover was a hand-drawn stack of pinecones and a mound of miniature twigs of fresh thyme.

'I'm definitely taking this book on holiday and I'm going to solve the mystery of the sparkling letters and symbols. Maybe the clue is in the title and I will find the answer in Provence,' Sevi said, very excitedly.

Sevi looked at her hands and saw tiny fragments of glitter coiled in circles on her palms. She discovered not only the coils of glitter, but also that her fingertips were lightly smudged with charcoal. Red-faced she pulled a hairband from her pocket and roughly pulled her hair into a short ponytail, leaving traces of glitter amongst the fine wisps of her wavy hair. Then without much success, she tried to wipe the charcoal from her fingers by rubbing them onto her jeans. 'Oops, better not let Mum see me do that!' Sevi said, swallowing her words.

Sevi clutched the book firmly in her hands and looked at it one last time before carefully placing it inside her backpack, which she had left by the doorway.

'How did I remove the hand-drawn bug? I only touched it for a second. Umm, and as for the wings flickering, did I really imagine that? What's more,

where did the glitter come from?' said a very confused Sevi, as she went in search of her parents.

The conservatory lights twinkled a little longer before the timer switch turned their starry sparkle to sleep mode. The book jiggled at the bottom of Sevi's backpack; the bookshelves of the cosy stone-walled cottage had been its home for many, many years.

That night, Sevi's dad loaded his camper van with luggage for their family holiday. He picked up the backpack from outside the reading room on his final sweep for holiday items and tucked it underneath a rear passenger seat.

'Did you find a book to take?' Sevi's dad asked her.

'Umm, yeah, I did,' replied Sevi, with the feeling of butterflies in her tummy.

Later that night the family set off. Sevi's head nuzzled into a squishy cushion, and with her body wrapped in fleecy blankets she slept propped up on the rear bench seat next to her mum, who gave back seat directions to Sevi's dad whenever the satnav took them the wrong way.

During many dream-filled miles, the violet book with its jumble of letters and symbols flashed behind Sevi's sleeping eyes. Tiny bugs weaved in and out of butterfly nets in their efforts to escape capture, and the image of the winged bug from the front cover buzzed in and out of Sevi's dreams, but never stayed longer than a nanosecond. Buzzzzz.

Sevi and her parents travelled for several hours before they reached the undersea rail tunnel, which took them by train to France. When they arrived at

a northern French town, they rested properly. The town had a large square, several cafés, shops and a church with a bell tower.

After their rest, Sevi and her parents continued their journey south. They stopped at an old medieval village that was perched on a hilltop and overlooking a river. Later they visited walled cities with fairy-tale moated castles that clung to cliff tops sprinkled with tiny mauve flowers. They drove along country roads where light beige mottled plane trees folded their green-leafed branches like a tunnel above the camper van as it chugged along.

The family found their small holiday house nestled in a valley of grapevines and pine forests. It had terracotta roof tiles, cream outer walls, green wooden shutters, black coach lights and a pergola. There was a sweet-water stream with a row of plane trees behind it and a circle of four-hundred-year-old olive trees at the front.

Sevi, in her crumpled clothes and with fingers of faded charcoal, slept soundly as her dad carried her from the camper van to the soft feather mattress of the holiday house.

As Sevi turned in her sleep, tiny flecks of golden glitter tumbled over her pillow. She dreamt of warm adventure-filled days that started with fresh pastries, soft berry jams, fruit juices and bowls of piping hot chocolate. All too soon, a tiny glimmer of sunlight peeped through the edges of the closed shutters as she stirred from her sleep.

With a start, Sevi's eyes opened wide as she remembered the violet book. Jumping out of bed,

she unlatched the shutters to get her first daylight view of white limestone mountains and poppy-filled meadows.

Blue chaser dragonflies hovered outside the window, their wings making a cracking noise as they dipped in the air.

With the book grasped in her hands, Sevi rushed to the terrace hoping to join her parents for breakfast. Her mum sat at the table drinking coffee from a cup, which Sevi thought looked not much bigger than an egg cup. Sevi's dad, who had already eaten, stood by the olive trees admiring the view. Smiling, Sevi waved at her dad. She sat and stared out towards the grapevines with her hands clutching a bowl of piping hot chocolate.

Ants marched their way up the wall of the terrace and went in search of pastry crumbs that had fallen from the family's breakfast napkins.

As Sevi's fingers opened the book's violet cover, a cuckoo broke into song from a pine tree branch and cigales buzzed nearby. Sevi looked at the gold-edged pages and wondered if she would ever decode the violet book.

CHAPTER 2

CHARLIE AND HIS FOREST FRIENDS

The pheasant stood on the dusty dirt track with his head raised. His black head, with a dash of red, looked as striking as the poppies that grew in the nearby meadow. With the rising of the sun Corinne, a common cuckoo, made her early-morning call across the valley, waking her sleepy forest friends.

'Sore, soooo sorezzz! My throat is sore,' buzzed Charlie.

Charlie, an adventure seeking, sneezing, flying bug with bulging eyes and lattice wings was one of a couple of dozen rare breed cigales who suffered greatly with allergies. Charlie's distinctive nose set him apart from regular cigales, not only did he have a nose that was most noticeable, it usually glowed raspberry red and apple green.

Charlie spent his days sneezing, snuffling and daydreaming of faraway places. Although Charlie had never flown further than the stream that flowed alongside the row of plane trees behind Sevi's holiday house, it never stopped him daydreaming of one day spreading his wings and seeing the world.

Charlie's allergies had kept him awake all night, his eyelids felt heavy and his nose was very sore. With a yawn he flew down to pick up a sprig of thyme from a store he had at the base of his favourite pine tree. He used the tiny leaves of this delicate herb as tissues to wipe his allergy-prone nose.

Gisele, a lime-green grasshopper, had just completed ten press-ups at the "Limestone Grasshopper Gym". She desperately needed help with her breathing exercises. The heat sapped most of her energy; she found it a struggle to exercise. She had also eaten too many blades of grass recently; her "hourgrass" figure needed toning up. 'Heh, Charlie, don't tell the hoppers, but I need help with my breathing exercises and there is no bug better qualified to teach me than you, so will you help?' Gisele asked.

'Help! You want me, a cigale, to help? Buzzing bananas! I'll have to think about it, Gisele. I'm a bit busy at the moment,' said Charlie, with a glowing face and even rosier nose.

'You are "Master Cigale" after all,' replied Gisele, looking rather disappointed.

Charlie made incredibly fast breathing movements in warm weather and this is how he won his title of Master Cigale. Whenever he breathed fast he buzzed and clicked very loudly.

When crowned Master Cigale twelve months ago at the "Bugsect Multi-Buzz Championship" the Committee for Cigales suggested Charlie competed against Spanish cicadas. His training had gone remarkably well until he collided belly-first with a plane tree. With badly bruised muscles, Charlie was unable to compete.

Charlie needed to start re-training for the following year's competition, but as the weeks went by, he spent more and more time in the forest, daydreaming about travel and adventure.

'Buzz, achoo, buzz, achoo.' Charlie's buzzes and sneezes were evenly spaced, which made him sound like a one-bug band.

Out of all the allergy-prone cigales or Snuffle-Buzzers (as they were also known), Charlie was the most tuneful. Sometimes his forest friends called him Sneezlybuzzlebug, because he often combined a sneeze with a buzz.

Charlie's throat still itched and felt like it was under attack from a pine needle.

'Deliciouszzz,' Charlie said, as he slurped his breakfast sap hoping that it would soothe his throat. 'Still sore, soooo very sorezzz,' said Charlie, with a little flushed face. 'If only the old winegrower was here, I am sure he could help me and the other Snuffle-Buzzers. Achoo!' Charlie flapped his wings and sorrowfully shook his head.

Charlie's trusty friends watched his frenzied actions as he wiped his eyes with his delicate wings.

After a night of foraging for mushrooms, berries and fruits, Hervé, a wild boar, and his family returned to their den (a disused military pillbox). Olivier, a graceful owlfly dressed in yellow and black, stretched his wings and flew towards his unflappable friend, Stephanie, a stick insect. Stephanie stirred from her branch and scooped a drop of water from a dampened lush-green leaf.

Charlie and his friends lived happily together within the forest, where the smell of yellow broom bushes and the sound of birdsong filled the air.

Orange and auburn coloured butterflies zigzagged along the forest pathways. Crickets dived into a pile of parched leaves near to three white fluffy dandelion heads that swayed gently in the breeze. Black millipedes, like strips of liquorice, tiptoed soundlessly over earth and stone. Blankets of cobwebs sprinkled with dust clung to the rough edges of the dirt track where the pheasant had stood earlier that morning.

'Buzz, achoo, buzz, achoo,' spluttered Charlie, as the sweet scent of wild orchids made his nose twitch.

'Poor old Sneezlybuzzlebug. Look here, you will make the pine leaves quiver, quiver I say,' said Corinne, flying down from a pine tree. She pecked a thyme leaf from Charlie's supply and wiped his nose for him.

'I'll miss you, Corinne, when you leave for British shores,' sniffled Charlie. 'No one looks after me like you do!'

'Oh, Charlie, you have many friends here and I will return to see you. I promise I will come home to my beloved friends,' chirped Corinne.

Suddenly an idea popped into Charlie's head, but it was at the same time as an allergic sneeze developed. 'Can I achoovel with you?' Charlie blurted his request so fast that Corinne turned her head to one side.

'I say, I didn't quite catch that,' said Corinne.

'I would like to achoovel with you?' said Charlie, sneezing and snuffling.

Corinne still looked confused.

'Can I travel with you? Pleasezzz,' buzzed Charlie.

Charlie crossed his wings over his raspberry red and apple green nose, hopeful that Corinne would take him with her.

'Oh, Charlie, Master Cigale, it is far too dangerous, far too dangerous. No, no, no. What would your ma-cigale or grand-cigale say? No, no it is quite out of the question. Impossible, no!'

'It's because I'm a sneezing cigale isn't it?'

'No, no, not at all. You have your whole life to experience adventure flights, no rush, no rush I say. I'll discuss it with your ma-cigale another time,' chirped Corinne.

'I'm already middle cigale-grade, and I haven't flown further than the streamzzz or the row of plane trees. Talking of plane trees, if I hadn't collided belly-first with that pesky plane tree I would have gone to Spain. I would have shown them cicadas a buzz or two. Instead, I messed everything up because next time they are coming here. How is a Snuffle-Buzzer ever to spread his wings?' grumbled Charlie.

'Charlie, Charlie, it has nothing at all to do with your sneezing and snuffling, let alone your buzzing, or clicking or messing anything up. It is because you are my dearest friend. I say my dearest friend and I want you to keep safe. That means staying here where thyme leaves and pine trees are plentiful. This is your home,' explained Corinne. 'Besides, Charlie, there is plenty of time for you to travel once you have re-trained for the Bugsect Multi-Buzz Championship against the Spanish cicadas.'

'Bugsect Multi-Buzz Championship!' repeated Charlie, with a sinking heart and a loud gulp.

Charlie stood still, head low and wings by his side. He had spent so much time daydreaming he had forgotten all about the re-training. 'Buzzing bananas! Rare breed cigales only live for a few years, I think I'd rather spend my time travelling not training,' said Charlie with a heavy sigh, as he flew towards an opening in the soil where his grand-cigale lived.

CHAPTER 3

THE MISTRAL AND THE CIGALE DISCOVERY

Six villagers, each wearing hats to protect them from the sun, knelt on rubble and rocks as they expertly counted and nipped the stems of the grapevines. Charlie snuffled as he left his grand-cigale's home and flew amongst the vine leaves that had a faint smell of rotten eggs. 'Poooohhh, achoo,' said Charlie. The sulphur mould spray, although a little smelly, was a perfect treatment for the grapevines. Thin-legged spiders and stripy wasps buried themselves under the vine leaves and were not at all bothered.

In the back bedroom of the holiday house Sevi had finally unpacked. Without noticing that her orange wash sponge was still in her suitcase, she closed the tatty and torn lid then pushed the case underneath the bedroom window, before heading to the bathroom. As with Sevi's favourite old suitcase, the orange wash sponge had seen better days. A small decorative hand rope through the centre of the sponge had stretched the holes, forming deep orange pockets.

'Ouch, shampoo in my eyes! Where's my wash sponge?' Sevi said aloud. Her fingers were now clean from the charcoal that had stained her skin, and soapy suds of shampoo had washed the glitter out of her wavy hair.

Sevi returned to her bedroom and opened the violet book. 'I'm never going to be able to understand these codes and symbols. There's not even another sketch inside of the winged bug. What a pity. He looked a cool dude of a bug. I'd get top grades if I could draw him for art class. I wonder how we came by this book in the first place. Very strange,' said Sevi.

Sevi lowered her head, and once more flicked through the gold-edged pages, when suddenly a cool breeze whirled around the bedroom freezing her to the spot. With a brilliant flash of light, the violet book dropped from her hands and landed on her bed. 'Eh, where did that come from?' asked Sevi, as she looked in bewilderment around the room.

'Sevi, are you ready yet? Come on, let's go before the weather sets in,' called her mum.

'Just coming,' Sevi shouted back as she looked over her shoulder at the violet book with its spine of flashing purple letters. 'Wild! This book appears to have a mind of its own.'

Sevi set off in search of her butterfly net and in her haste left the bedroom window partly open. The bedroom became calm again, except for a slight rattle that came from the shutters.

'It's looking a bit dull,' Sevi said, as she gazed upwards.

Sevi picked up her butterfly net and met her parents by the side of the pergola. She liked to look closely, but always briefly, at the colourful markings on the delicate wings of butterflies.

Olivier darted haphazardly around the forest. Looking up, he too noticed that the blue sky had changed to ash-grey. His black and yellow coat no longer glistened. It was as though the sun had placed a pair of sunglasses on its face and decided to take a nap.

An eerie darkness loomed over the valley and a forceful wind blew amongst the wild orchids. However, the ash-grey sky did not discourage the family and so they headed off for their ramble. Sevi's dad carried a map, compass and a small digital camera in his pocket. All three had Nordic walking poles and drinking water.

The family walked along rocky forest trails and climbed a twisty, steep pathway that led to a ridge with a view over the valley. Beyond the row of plane trees, near to their holiday house, they stopped to watch the stream as it flowed beneath a curved stone bridge. Perched midway up a hillside, near to a field with grazing sheep, stood a shuttered house. Behind its wrought iron gates, a garden of colourful wildflowers swayed in front of a terrace where an open-topped oak barrel rested on six rusty wheels.

The gusty wind chased the three ramblers along the limestone pathways of the craggy mountain, making all three walk much faster.

Squelch, squelch, and squish. Sevi nearly succeeded in jumping over a huge mud puddle, but splattered her boots in sticky gloop. 'This is great, look at the animal paw prints in here,' she said, hopping onto the dry clay edge.

The wind blew against Sevi's face as she waved her butterfly net into the air and left the mud puddle to a cloud of gnats. She didn't mind that her hair became messed up or that she would have to clean her boots; she loved outdoor life.

With the mountainside covered in shadow, the family stopped briefly under the canopy of a cedar tree. Sevi delved into her backpack and pulled out a white paper bag. 'Excellent, clotted cream sweets!' said Sevi, with a huge smile on her face.

The ramble brought the family full circle back down to the lower forest trails, where Stephanie was motionless and completely camouflaged on a section of bark. Sevi and her parents trekked by the stone pillbox; nothing stirred within. Small, unevenly shaped rocks and gravel crunched under the family's boots as they walked along the limestone trail. The spikes of their Nordic walking poles pierced the soft ground, and all the while the wind blew and blew.

Corinne's song echoed in the distance. As she soared into a bank of cloud, it muted her call. 'Cuckoo, cuckoo, cuck, cuc, cu, cu.'

Bracken and twisted tree roots spread over much of the forest floor. Red and black ladybirds picnicked either on pollen or the mildew that had grown upon a felled tree trunk.

'Olivier, Olivier, where are you?' called Charlie, as he flew towards a sweeping pine tree branch in search of his owlfly friend.

As Sevi rambled through the forest, miniature bugs

crashed against her face before their tiny bodies fell into her yellow butterfly net.

When Olivier spotted Charlie, struggling to hold onto a nearby tree trunk, two different types of click filled the forest air; one click was from Charlie and the other from a camera.

Tall sweeping branches struck the pillbox, waking Hervé and his family of wild boars. Hervé poked his head out of the pillbox, but did not venture outside.

In the heart of the forest, the bells from a Roman chapel rang on the hour. The mauve and grey sky above the chapel looked as angry as a giant bruise. The dark clouds rolled by as though knitting a cloud blanket that crossed the valley and met with the coast.

The strong wind blew across the poppy-filled meadow, causing the branches of the almond trees to scrape the dust on the dirt track. 'I'm out of here. It's too blowy for me,' said Gisele, as her bright green body dashed from the meadow to the grapevines. There she took shelter under a leaf of a goblet vine.

The Mistral had returned.

The family completed their forest ramble a little after midday. They stopped at a small café with a red sunshade and an arched wooden doorway that led through to a low-ceilinged room with round oak tables and high-back chairs. During their lunch of fish soup and crusty bread, they sat listening to the terracotta roof tiles as they clinked and clanked with each gust of wind.

'I didn't realise the Mistral could be this fierce, Dad,' Sevi said. 'I think it's wild and very exciting, but

I hope it doesn't last for days. I want us to make the most of our holiday and be able to go out and about.'

Charlie had flown from the forest to an Aleppo pine, which overlooked Sevi's bedroom at the holiday house. The mighty wind caused Charlie's bug eyes to water, and as he wiped the droplets away he noticed that the window to Sevi's bedroom was slightly open.

Charlie caught his breath and pressed his wings hard against the side of the tree.

'How am I ever going to hatch a travel plan with this raging wind? I can't think straight and I really need to come up with a plan soon!' Charlie shouted.

All the while the Mistral blew stronger, the sky grew darker and Charlie gripped the pine tree tighter.

The smell of rotten eggs from the vine leaves wafted towards Charlie. 'Buzz, achoo, buzz, achoo. Great, here come my allergies. Perfect timing! Achoo!'

Charlie tried with all of his might to stay attached to the puzzle-blocked bark. His body rocked back and forth until eventually, Charlie lost his grip. The strong gusty wind lifted him up and off the tree. At first Charlie felt thrilled by the upward motion, but soon his head felt fuzzy. 'Helppp meezzz,' Charlie cried, but the wind carried the sound of the cigale. 'Whoa, whoa!' he cried, once more.

A very powerful gust pushed Charlie towards the holiday house. One huge blast of air released the latch of a shutter from its cradle; it banged loudly against the outer wall. The open window that Sevi had left ajar opened further and beckoned Charlie.

The Mistral hurtled Charlie, bedraggled and

defeated, through the open window where he finally landed on Sevi's torn suitcase.

The Mistral had won.

Inside the dimly lit bedroom, an earwig nudged close to the skirting board then crawled out of sight behind the suitcase.

Charlie raised one of his shaking wings and mopped several teardrops that sprung from his eyes. Charlie's battle with the forceful wind had frightened and exhausted him, but he still managed to mutter a few words before he fell asleep. 'Why did I choose to hatch another travel plan in the middle of a wind storm? Maybe Corinne is right, perhaps I should stay here and train for the championship. Whilst I am at it, I should work on how to keep my grasp on a pine tree. I must have looked like a wobbling gollywhopper,' choked Charlie.

Battered, bruised and very downhearted, Charlie fell fast asleep dreaming once again of faraway places. As Charlie slept, he gently slipped through the tattered fabric of the suitcase and sunk into Sevi's soft, orange wash sponge.

On the white duvet cover the violet book, with its spine of purple letters, codes, symbols and puzzling words, sparkled brighter than ever before. This caused Charlie's wings to glow with a very pale shade of violet.

Charlie's friends sheltered throughout the forest and vineyard during the Mistral. It was not until calm returned to the valley and the late afternoon sunshine peeped through the tall pine trees that the forest friends started their search for him.

'I have searched vine upon vine, pine upon pine and I cannot find him. I say vine and pine, but still no sign of Charlie,' chirped Corinne whose beak chattered with worry. 'Let us all search some more, I say more searches are in order. I hope he has not flown off and got into difficulty. I will never forgive myself, I say never forgive! I told him he could not travel with me, worried for his safety, I say worried for him and now he is missing at home. Charlie, where are you? Cuckoo, cuckoo.'

After her ramble, Sevi carried a glass of strawberry juice into her bedroom and placed it on the bedside cabinet. Sevi found the room to be warm, so she strolled over to open the window. 'Already open. Oops, I forgot to close it.' Bending down, she picked up a handful of twigs, threw them outside, and then took a sip of juice.

Suddenly within the stillness of the room, she heard a buzzy-click. 'Oh no, oh no, I've let a critter in!' Sevi glanced around the room, but it looked the same as she had left it.

'Buzz, buzz, buzz, buzz, buzz.'

Pulling a hairband from her pocket Sevi tied her hair into a ponytail. She knelt down on her hands and knees and crooked her neck to check underneath the bed. There she spotted the amber coloured earwig as it slinked over a square white tile. 'Umm, that's not the buzzing bug,' said Sevi, as she listened out for another buzz.

It was then that Sevi realised the buzzing seemed to be coming from her suitcase. Frowning, she walked over to the tatty case and paused before she bent down and peered inside. There, wedged in between the hollowed orange pockets of her wash sponge, stood Charlie, Master Cigale.

'Buzzzzz.'

Quickly, Sevi jumped up from the floor and closed the bedroom door before her parents heard the commotion.

Sevi had already heard the buzzy-clicks that came with warm days and airless nights, however, the sight of one of these buzzing bugs was most unfamiliar to Sevi, or was it? On a second look, there was something familiar about the winged creature, something most familiar indeed!

Sevi slumped on the bed and stared at Charlie. Slightly embarrassed and confused, Charlie returned Sevi's gaze. Charlie raised a wing to hide his reddening face then, brushing it quickly over his head, he remembered his defeat against the fierce Mistral.

'Hoopla,' said Charlie, as he struggled to clamber out of the wash sponge. Standing straight, he stretched his wings and flew around the room.

With her jaw almost on the floor, Sevi called, 'Whoa, what did you say and where are you going?'

Charlie landed gently on the violet cover of Sevi's book, causing the pages to rustle.

'Flung through the window, the Mistral, it wasn't my fault. I was trying to think of a way to have adventures and seezzz a foreign land,' rambled Charlie.

'I really am no trouble, but Corinne, that's my very

best cuckoo friend, will not take me with her on her travels. For my own safety she thinks I should stay here in the forest.

'I am supposed to re-train for the Bugsect Multi-Buzz Championship. Oh, you won't know, but it's a fast breathing competition and I have to compete against Spanish cicadas.' Very briefly, Charlie stopped talking and fixed his eyes on the violet book.

'I am capable of looking after myself. I'm grown up now! I'm middle cigale-grade. I only need a chance to spread my wings!' exclaimed Charlie.

Charlie took another gasp of air and wiggled his wings. Sevi sat watching Charlie. Her hands became clammy, her heart raced and her eyes followed Charlie's every move as he twitched, sneezed and fluttered his wings, that were still a shade of pale violet.

Charlie's fast, rattling speech bewildered Sevi, but she listened carefully to everything the winged creature said. He spoke so fast he did not give Sevi a chance to say anything!

'OK, to be honest I am a bit of an allergy sufferer, you know snuffle and sneeze, but my supply of thyme leaves and tree sap usually takes care of that. Oh, I am buzzing on and on. Sorry! I am not supposed to be here, my friendszzz will wonder where I am. Sorry for any inconveniencezzz. Byezzz,' buzzed Charlie, as he sprung up and took flight.

Sevi jumped and with both hands reached out; she tried to prevent Charlie from escaping.

Charlie darted around the room then landed for the second time on the cover of the book. He rested on the spot where the artist had drawn a pine tree. This time not only did the pages rustle and the cover twinkle like a diamond tiara, the sprigs of thyme flashed with a purple glow. 'Wow,' Sevi said, looking at the book in astonishment. 'Double wow!' Sevi smiled and excitedly clapped her hands several times against her legs. 'I know why you seem familiar. You are the real thing, the real deal. You are the exact same winged bug that was drawn in charcoal on the cover of this book!' With her fingertips, Sevi tapped the cover next to where Charlie sat.

'Yes, I'm Charlie, a cigale, but not just any old cigale. I am a rare breed allergy-prone one, also known as a Snuffle-Buzzer. I was born and bred in this pine forest! I am very happy living here with my family and friendszzz, but I desperately want to have my share of adventure-filled travel before time runs out,' said Charlie, at breakneck speed, pointing his wings towards the open window.

Charlie breathed heavily, buzzing and clicking, as he stared at the cover of the book. He remained focused on the cover until Sevi spoke.

'Oh, so you're a Snuffle-Buzzer! Well hello, Charlie. I'm Sevi. Can I ask what do you mean before time runs out?'

Charlie sprung up, whipped a small thyme leaf out from underneath one of his wings, blew his nose and buzzed loudly. 'Some cigales can live for up to seventeen years, but not us. Rare breed allergy-prone cigales only live for a few years. That's why I want to make the most of my life,' replied Charlie, his eyes once more staring hard at the cover of the book.

Sevi frowned, realising how important it was for Charlie to seek travel and adventure.

As Charlie fluttered around the room, his bug eyes concentrated on the violet cover. At the very moment when Charlie landed on the book, for the third time, shards of tri-coloured glitter exploded from the violet cover. The sparkles whizzed around Charlie's head and then fell silently upon the crisp, white duvet cover.

'Glitter on the duvet, oh no!' exclaimed Sevi. 'What's going on with this book? It's sparkling like crazy. What's more, I can't understand a word of it! I've been trying to work it out ever since I found it on our bookshelves at home!'

Charlie blinked then slowly turned his head to look at his wings.

'Hey, Charlie, your wings are flashing super-violet!' said Sevi. 'This is wild! What's happening and how is it that we can understand each other?'

CHAPTER 4

UNLEASHING THE GLITTERING POWERS

'Buzzing bananas! I'll tell you what's going on! It's trying to unleash glittering powers! Advanced Cigale-language, that's what the book has been written in. There are also codes, symbols and charms sealed within this book,' said a very happy Charlie, as he flapped his violet wings.

'Glittering powers and advanced Cigale-language? As if I know what they are,' replied Sevi.

'Glittering powers? That's a longer story. Cigale-language is simply our language. In all cigale history there has only been one human able to understand an advanced version of Cigale-language, and he was a man of mystique.'

'How do you know what is in the book? You haven't looked inside yet!' asked Sevi.

'These big eyes aren't just to make me look handsome! Rare breed cigales have Xzzz-ray paper vision, so I have taken a few quick peeks through the cover. Mind you, I'm only middle cigale-grade at cigale-school, still learning all this stuff. My grand-cigale knows Cigale-language in-soil and out,' replied Charlie, as he thought of his grand-cigale sitting underground, soil up to his bug eyes, studying advanced Cigale-language and codes.

'I thought middle cigale-grade was grown up?' asked Sevi, with a raised eyebrow.

'Well, yes it is sort of, but this is, umm different. As I said these codes are advanced,' replied Charlie, with a rosy glow to his cheeks.

Charlie's bug eyes kept staring at the book; it was as though he was waiting for something, some kind of signal. Suddenly a popping and cracking noise came from the book, shortly followed by a golden light that beamed brightly around the room.

'Oh now what?' asked Sevi. With panic and excitement, Sevi started to wave her hands in the air.

One single golden sparkle from Charlie's glowing raspberry red and apple green nose signalled to him that his glittering powers had been fully unleashed!

Charlie flew quickly to the centre of Sevi's right palm. He hopped about, flapped his wings three times and sneezed very loudly. 'Achoo!' However, Charlie's sneeze was no ordinary sneeze; it appeared to be a sneeze of glittering sparkles.

Sevi looked incredibly puzzled when she saw Charlie sneeze a fountain of glitter. 'Oh my days! You've just sneezed glitter. I can't believe it. Well at least your wings are no longer super-violet!' she said, glancing at Charlie's flushed face and natural-coloured lattice wings.

'Whoo hoo! My glittering powers have been fully unleashed and it's all thanks to you for returning the violet book! Today is an historic day for all Provençal Snuffle-Buzzers. Soon all new generations of our rare breed will have glittering powers! Oh and, Sevi, it has been yearszzz since a young overseas traveller has had a sneezing cigale land on their right palm,' said Charlie, thrilled with how his day was panning out.

Sevi gulped her strawberry juice. 'Charlie, this is all brilliant, but before you go any further, I still don't know how it's possible for us to understand each other!' said Sevi.

'It is in the mix, Sevi! It is in the mix. The glittering powers from the violet book and a sneezing cigale on the palm of a young overseas traveller allow both the cigale and the traveller to talk to each other,' explained Charlie. 'Anyway, I think that is what my grand-cigale said!'

'But I could understand you before you did your wing flapping, sneezing dance on my right palm,' said Sevi.

'I know, but the mix is very powerful and from the moment I fell on top of your suitcase, which was near to the violet book, the charms sealed within the book started to transfer some of their mystical glittering powers to me. This enabled us to talk to each other,' Charlie said, very excitedly. 'But, if I hadn't landed on the violet cover my full glittering powers would never have been unleashed.'

'Well it's a good job you landed on the cover three times!' said Sevi.

'Yes it was! Then, when I did my "wing flapping, sneezing dance", as you put it, on your right palm, the glittering powers made sure that after tomorrow's sunrise we would still be able to understand each other,' explained Charlie. 'Remember, Sevi, it is in the mix.'

'I don't think I will ever forget,' Sevi replied, looking utterly surprised.

'I really have my glittering powers – excellentzzz! I've just had a thought. Can you carry the book to the forest for me?' asked Charlie, with glitter sprinkled upon his wings.

'Yes, of course. I know the book is small, but it is still a lot bigger than you!' said Sevi.

The enchanted twinkling glitter rose from the duvet cover and vanished through the window, leaving Sevi to wonder where it would go.

CHAPTER 5

THE MIX

'Will we always be able to understand each other?' asked Sevi.

'Umm, I'm not sure. I hope so, but over time the glittering powers may have other ideas,' replied Charlie. 'We will have to wait and seezzz.'

'OK. I'd like to know about the mix and the glittering powers, but first what or who is a grand-cigale?' Sevi asked.

'A grand-cigale is like your grandfather, and ma-cigale is the same as your mother,' said Charlie.

Charlie rather liked teaching Sevi things that she did not know; it made him feel very grown up and important.

'Has your grand-cigale told you many stories from years gone by?' asked Sevi.

'Yes, he buzzes to me all the time about life here in the forest, but the most important story that stickszzz firmly in my memory, and in the memorieszzz of all other allergy suffering cigales is the tale of the old winegrower. Get comfy, Sevi, and I'll tell you all that I know,' buzzed Charlie.

Sevi sipped more of her strawberry juice, propped herself up against the carved pinewood headboard and listened carefully to what Charlie had to say.

'Many years ago, an old winegrower who lived on this vineyard grew fine grapes, which he made into wines of rich reds and pastel pinks. He spent his lunchtimes in the forest under the shade of pine tree branches, or by the Roman chapel studying rare breed Snuffle-Buzzers. One spring day when the ground temperature became very high, an allergy-prone cigalative of mine scrambled out of the soil and landed on the hands of the old winegrower. As the winegrower sat on a narrow limestone ledge, behind the Roman chapel, he watched as she snuffled and sneezed. Distressed by her sneezing, he felt that something needed to be done to help her and other Snuffle-Buzzers.'

'Charlie, I have a question. Was the man of mystique the old winegrower?'

'Yes, he was,' replied Charlie.

'Just one thing. Cigalative, is that the same as relative?'

'Yes, yes, you have the hang of it. Cigale-language is quirky, but has certain words that are similar to those in the English language. Then, as you discovered in the violet book, we have advanced Cigale-language with what appears to be a jumble of letters, but of course isn't. The thing is, Sevi, without the understanding of our advanced Cigale-language the codes, symbols and cigale folklore charms would be impossible to learn.'

'Phew! I wish I could learn it all,' said Sevi.

'It is very complicated! Anyway, as I was saying, the winegrower's desire to help Snuffle-Buzzers became overwhelming. He became friendszzz with my cigalative, Henny.'

'How did the winegrower learn advanced Cigale-language?'

'We are supposed to have our cigalessons underground, deep beneath the soil, but one sunny day, Henny dragged her selection of miniature Cigale-language books to the surfacezzz. The old winegrower grew very interested in the books and borrowed some from Henny. He worked incredibly hard to learn the language of rare breed cigales, and even harder to understand the codes, symbols and our folklore charms. Mind you, his knowledge of forest folklore charms and his mystical ability helped him greatly.

'Remember, glittering powers had yet to be created and so at that point Henny and the winegrower could not speak to each other,' said Charlie.

'Oh yeah,' Sevi said, as she pulled herself forward and wrapped her arms around her bent legs.

'So, in a small pocket-sized book, the violet book that you have here, the winegrower set about creating a world of glittering powers that would help Henny and the other Snuffle-Buzzers.'

'Wild,' said Sevi. 'So what did he do to help?'

'Every night the winegrower left his housezzz to go to an old military pillbox in the forest. Into an open-topped oak barrel, he mixed the juice of grapezzz with the dye from the petals of Provençal wildflowers. He even placed the small book, which he had sealed with mystical cigale and forest folklore charms, inside the barrel, and yet he could not get the mixture right. Because of this, he removed the book and sealed even more mystical cigale folklore charms within it.

'It was on a night when the Mistral blew and a half-moon lit an eerie glow over the poppy fields that he finally knew what he needed to add to the mixture. He quickly placed the small book in his pocket and once more headed to the forest. He hobbled down the hill, under the wings of screeching owls, over the dusty dirt track and along the pale moonlit trails towards the pillbox. Just as the chapel bells rung eleven o'clock, he collected his secret ingredient. Into the barrel, once more, he added grape juice, petal dye, the book and finally a sprinkling of his secret ingredient. At last it was ready.'

'So this is what you call the mix!' said Sevi. 'It's exciting, it's exciting.'

'Buzz, buzz, buzz. Exactly right!' replied Charlie, as he gasped for air.

'What happened next?' Sevi stretched her legs and picked up the book.

'The old winegrower had attached a set of six wheels to the base of the barrel which made it easier for him to roll over the uneven floor of the dark pillbox. Sevi, the wheels came in handy because when the mix splattered and popped so high that it hit the roof, he was able to push the barrel with its sparkling enchanted mix onto the limestone pathway. Violet, purple and gold sparks soared high above the pine tree forest, streaming glittering flakes up towards the stars.

The cigale folklore charms finally released a beam of golden light that shone brightly against the sapphire blue sky. The book spun in the air and with one final swirl drifted downwards where it landed close to a stack of pinecones at the entrance to the pillbox.'

'Amazing,' said Sevi.

'Yes, and all the cigales raised their heads to watch the light show. With a dazzling explosion of colour, the sparkling glitter tumbled like a horsetail firework through the tall trees. The twinkling glitter fell onto the small book, casting a mystical violet dye onto the cover and sealing within the gold-edged pages super-charms that could unleash glittering powers for Snuffle-Buzzers.

'With the light display over and the glittering powers created, the old winegrower picked up the violet book and on the front cover he sketched a picture of a cigale on a pine tree,' said Charlie, glancing at the violet book.

'Ah, the charcoal cigale!' said Sevi. 'So, the glittering powers of the violet book were created in this pine forest; then why did I find the book at my home in Cornwall?'

CHAPTER 6

THE LOST VIOLET BOOK

'There is more to the story,' replied Charlie. 'One day, long after the explosive mix had cast its mystical charms and the Snuffle-Buzzers were snuffle and sneezezzz free, the winegrower sat underneath a cedar tree, high on the upper crag with the newly charmed book in his hands. The Snuffle-Buzzers buzzed loudly; they were very happy with their glittering powers. But, with the old winegrower's new understanding of cigale folklore charms, he thought he would dabble a little further making the glittering powers even greater.'

'But why change a winning recipe?' asked Sevi.

'I don't know, and unfortunately something terrible happened. Whilst planning a new mix he fell asleep, and as he slept the Mistral arrived. With one almighty gust of wind the violet book fell from his open hands over the side of the white rocky crag to the forest trail below,' said Charlie.

'Oh no! What happened next?' asked Sevi.

'The winegrower used multiple forest folklore charms in his search for the violet book, but sadly

35

never found it. Rumour has it the glittering powers sealed within the book, tempora, temp, tempora…'

'Temporarily,' Sevi said, helping Charlie out.

'Buzzing bananas! Yes, that's the word! They, umm, shut down for a little while, which made it difficult for the old winegrower to track down the book!'

'I see. A bit like Mum's mobile. She never gets a signal when she needs one,' said Sevi.

'I don't know what a mobile is, but I do know that I never thought I'd seezzz the book in my lifetime. I cannot tell you how excizzzted I am,' said Charlie, as he adjusted his lattice wings so their curved folds touched neatly along the middle of his back.

'Grand-cigale told me that Henny, who by the way was the very first Snuffle-Buzzer to have her glittering powers unleashed, befriended a young boy from overseas. He too had experienced the wing flapping, sneezing dance on his right palm.

'Henny asked the boy to help her find the missing book. Intrigued by Henny's description of the codes, symbols and advanced Cigale-language, he eagerly searched throughout the valley and along the limestone pathways. On a bright sun-filled day, whilst searching, the boy stumbled over some thorny bracken. There amongst the bracken, close to a pile of knobbly pinecones, he spied a sparkling violet cover. He had found the book!'

'Charlie, this boy…' Sevi started to ask Charlie a question, but keen to complete his tale, he rattled on.

'Henny had watched, from a pine tree not far from the pillbox, as the boy clambered free from the thorn-filled bracken. He opened the violet cover and, with a guilty look, he quickly closed the cover and placed the book inside his pocket. Before Henny could tell the old winegrower, the boy with the violet book had left the forest. Henny had said that the boy was kind but misguided.'

Charlie and Sevi sat quietly as a drop of dappled light splashed onto the book's violet cover. After a few minutes of silence Sevi spoke.

'Charlie, it's obvious, the boy you are talking about must be my dad. I knew my grandparents had taken him for boating holidays along French canals, but I didn't know he had also been to this pine forest. It really has to have been my dad who took the violet book, that's how I found it at home!' exclaimed Sevi shaking her head.

'Buzzzzz, buzzzzz, buzzzzz,' Charlie's raspberry red and apple green nose shone.

'Right, that settles it. My family owe you a huge favour! Charlie, I have the best idea ever! Seeing how it was my dad that has prevented all new generations of Snuffle-Buzzers from having glittering powers, I'm going to help you satisfy your dreams of travel and adventure.'

'Really, Sevi? How?'

'I'll take you home to Cornwall with me so you can have your first travel adventure,' said Sevi, smiling widely.

'Oh dear, it is getting warm in here,' buzzed a very thrilled Charlie.

Then just as Charlie thought all his dreams had come true...

'Warm, oh no. Warm means Bugsect Multi-Buzz training. Oh no.' Charlie dropped his head.

'Umm, that is a problem if you are going to return to Cornwall with me,' said Sevi, thoughtfully.

'Just my luck! After generations, Snuffle-Buzzers get their violet book back, I gain glittering powers, make a new friend and I am days away from adventure-filled travel only to have my dreams dashed.'

'Charlie, if you promise your family that you will return to your forest by late summer, so you can re-train for the championship, they might allow you to travel with me!' proposed Sevi.

'That is an excellentzzz solution!' said Charlie, hopping up and down.

'Better not tell my parents though. I'm guessing they won't think it's an excellent solution!' said Sevi, pondering how she would transport Charlie to Cornwall!

CHAPTER 7

THE CIGALE PINE TREE PARTY

Charlie, with his new glittering powers, flew around the bedroom madly flapping his wings. Breathless, he landed on top of the orange wash sponge. The sponge looked so inviting that Charlie burrowed himself back inside the cosy orange pockets. It was then that Sevi knew how she would transport Charlie to Cornwall.

After all the hullabaloo of the day, Sevi sighed and poked her head out of the window. Across the valley, she listened to the delightful tunes of birdsong. The Mistral waved goodbye with a promise to return another day.

'Well, the clue was in the title and I have found the answer here in Provence,' said Sevi, thinking back to when she first discovered the violet book on the wooden bookshelves at home.

Corinne searched by the stream for Charlie. On the grassy bank, close to the curved stone bridge, a family of large toads croaked loudly.

Two cats, one jet black and one tabby, rummaged for their supper, but only found crickets, gnats and small fruit flies in the long windswept meadow.

Sevi kept her discovery of Charlie and the book top secret. Looking at her dad at the dinner table, she knew he too had once discovered the glittering powers. Sevi finished dinner and stepped off the terrace. She watched the two cats scamper around the meadow and her thoughts returned to her dad. 'So you had an allergy-prone cigale friend too,' said Sevi, softly.

Sevi wondered why her dad had kept the book; over the years, he must have had at least one opportunity to return it to the Snuffle-Buzzers. She decided he probably kept it for the same reason that she wanted to take the book on holiday, and that was to solve the mystery of the codes, symbols and odd-looking words.

Sevi thought Henny had been right about her dad; he was kind, but had sadly been misguided.

Charlie played peek-a-boo with an earwig before leaving the comfort of the orange wash sponge. He flew through the open window back to the forest where a fusion of bats flittered and mingled in the night-time sky. The wild boars were about to set off on a night patrol to look for Charlie, when they spotted him dodging the fast-flying bats.

'I'm back. What a day I've had. You are never going to believe me!' said Charlie.

Charlie's family and forest friends were so very happy to see him. They all snuggled outside the pillbox where he told them of his recent escapade, the discovery of the mystical violet book and, of course, his meeting with Sevi and her offer of adventure-filled travel.

'I never thought I would ever have my glittering powers unleashed. My allergieszzz have disappeared. It is a miracle!' Charlie buzzed non-stop to all the Snuffle-Buzzers.

'You just wait until you get your glittering powers; it's so weird when you start sneezing glitter!' Charlie said, to a very young Snuffle-Buzzer. 'The glitter tickles your nose; it doesn't make your nose sorezzz or fuzzy like our allergy sneezes do. The gold glitter is something else!'

Charlie looked around to see an audience of rare breed cigales, with their wings fluttering and their bug eyes crying with joy.

'Sevi will bring the book here to the pillbox very soon, so you will seezzz for yourselves. From what I have heard the old winegrower sealed many charms within the book, so I can't wait to seezzz what else the glittering powers do,' said Charlie, looking at his grand-cigale. Charlie wanted him to be proud of his knowledge.

Charlie's newsreel was the best the forest creatures had heard in many years. News spread to Snuffle-Buzzers near and far and the forest was full of cigale chitter-chatter. The winged bugs flew from pine tree to pine tree slurping and sipping tree sap, buzzing and clicking and then slurping some more. They celebrated for many hours.

Charlie's family and friends were very proud of him. Charlie's grand-cigale wanted to reward Charlie for his find and asked him to name something he would like as a treat.

'Umm let me think, let me think!' Charlie said, pretending he did not know what to ask for. 'Well, you know Sevi offered to take me with her to Cornwall? If I promise to be back by late summer to re-train for the Bugsect Multi-Buzz Championship, can I go?' asked Charlie.

Charlie had everything crossed: his wings, his big bug eyes and his heartstrings. 'Before you say no just think, now that I have discovered the book, we won't need to take so many trips to the super-soil market to get frozen thyme and bottled sap for our throats and noseszzz,' Charlie said, in a very fast rattling voice.

All the Snuffle-Buzzers looked at each other smiling. To Charlie's delight his family agreed with his travel plans and did so with numerous buzzy-clicks. Their chitter-chatter kept the whole forest awake long after the bats had left the trees and headed for their home in the craggy mountainside caves.

Shortly before Charlie fell asleep, he looked up towards the sky with its half-moon and eerie glow. He crossed his wings and hoped that Sevi would keep her promise and not take the book, with its sealed glittering powers, home with her to Cornwall.

CHAPTER 8

GLITTERING TOFFEE APPLES

The long days that followed the family spent outdoors. The sun shone from dawn until dusk making streams shimmer and natural waterfalls burst to life. They canoed along milky-green waters surrounded by high-rise mountain gorges and trekked where wildflowers, prickly juniper, rosemary and thyme grew. They cycled through country roads where bundles of reeds swayed back and forth.

The family visited historic, medieval towns with old stone buildings. Towns with hundreds of fountains and cobbled streets received their footsteps. Narrow streets with arched alleyways welcomed the family, whom were desperate for afternoon shade.

Clean clothes, pegged to rows of wire and suspended from houses with shuttered windows, dried quickly from the heat.

Sevi saw abandoned dogs, ragged and lonely, lurking around street corners. She also saw miniature terriers, well-groomed and with coloured head ribbons, carried by their owners.

Up until his farewell, Charlie spent as much time

as possible getting to know his new friend, Sevi. Whenever Sevi went exploring with her parents, Charlie studied the violet book with its codes, symbols and advanced Cigale-language. Charlie made the most of his solo time with the violet book, allowing it to transfer more enchanted super-charms onto his lattice wings.

Sevi was late in her promise to carry the book to the forest. The Snuffle-Buzzers hadn't yet had their glittering powers unleashed; this had started to worry Charlie.

One evening, before Charlie left his pine forest to travel with Sevi, he went for an outing. Sevi sneaked him into an open pocket of her cargo trousers so Charlie could join her and her parents at a local funfair.

The night sky was ablaze with colour; fireworks whizzed and cracked in the sky. Charlie saw multi-coloured fairground rides that illuminated the park. The bright, noisy attractions enticed children, young and old, to join in. Throughout the fun-zone, the smell of sugar candy, fizzy pop, chocolate-dipped churros and hotdogs with caramelised fried onions and mustard wafted in the air.

Instead of birdsong and cigale chitter-chatter, Charlie heard pinging and pounding sounds from the funfair amusements.

'Buzzing bananas! This is great! My adventureszzz have already started.'

'Charlie, do you know what a banana is?' asked Sevi.

'Yes, of course, "ba-nana" that is what a sheep calls

his grand-ma-cigale,' said Charlie with a very cheeky look on his face.

'Ha! So do you think grandmothers buzz?' asked Sevi.

'Being a rare breed, mine does all the time. It drives me bananas!' said Charlie, laughing.

'I don't know about bananas, but I think I'd like a toffee apple,' said Sevi.

Sevi bought a toffee apple from a bearded man, whose stall was next to a pool with giant clear water balls. Sevi crunched and the glazed sugar coating of the toffee apple snapped under her bite. Whilst she was eating, Sevi had not realised that she was at the front of the queue for the water ball ride. Forced to place her half-eaten toffee apple back inside the cellophane wrapper, she crammed it into her cargo pocket, forgetting that Charlie was in there.

Within seconds, Sevi found herself inside an inflated transparent ball. It rolled over the water at great speed.

Inside Sevi's pocket, Charlie chuckled and flapped his wings, but as he did so the wrapper came free from the toffee apple and his wings stuck to the apple's sticky sugar coating. Charlie no longer chuckled! 'Urggghhhhhhhh buzz urgghhhh!' cried Charlie, but the noise from the funfair drowned out his buzzing urghs.

Sevi could not hear him.

The water ball rolled faster and faster. Charlie screamed louder and louder. His wings became stickier and stickier. Still the water ball rolled over and over the rippling water. Sevi managed to keep her balance until…

Bump!

The large transparent ball carrying Sevi and Charlie smashed with a thumping wallop into the centre of another rolling water ball. Sevi fell backwards and a very messy Charlie became detached from the toffee apple, which had made him look like a piece of crystallised stem ginger. Although no longer attached to the toffee apple, the sugary-glaze stuck firm to Charlie's wings.

As all the water balls finally rolled back to the starting point, Sevi prepared to leave her ball.

Charlie stuck his head out of her cargo pocket. 'Can you hear me? I'm really sticky and I look like a sugary sweet,' called Charlie.

Crowds of children were in line to take their turn for a go on the water ball ride. Sevi stepped out of her ball, a little wobbly, and sneaked behind the toffee apple stall.

'Hold still, Charlie, I'll help you,' said Sevi, still feeling a little unsteady.

Before Sevi had chance to remove the sugar coating from Charlie he sneezed – very loudly. His sneeze of glitter covered him from the top of his head to the bottom of his wings, removing all traces of the sticky glaze. Then quicker than one of Charlie's buzzy-clicks, the glitter swirled into the air and vanished from sight. 'Wow! These glittering powers aren't just for clearing up my allergieszzz!' buzzed Charlie.

'Are you alright, my little mate?' asked Sevi, as she popped Charlie back inside her cargo pocket.

'Yeszzz, I am finding these new powers most acceptabubble,' said Charlie, folding his wings behind him.

Under the smoke-filled sky a final batch of rocket fireworks, scarlet red, splintered high above the fairground rides, causing the crowds to ooh and ah.

With the noise of the funfair still ringing in their ears, the family walked along mountainside roads back to the vineyard where only starlight lit the sky. Sevi's parents strolled along the dusty dirt track. A few paces behind, Sevi quietly and very gently lifted Charlie out of her pocket. He flew, allergy free, over the vines and headed towards the pillbox. He spent his last night before his travels in the forest with his family and friends.

That night, long after Sevi's bedtime, she took the book from her tatty suitcase and looked at the brightly shining spine of purple letters. She let her imagination roam. Her eyes rolled over the codes, symbols and advanced Cigale-language, forever hopeful that one day she would be able to read it. 'I really should return this to the forest for Charlie, but it is so tempting to keep it for a little bit longer,' said Sevi, quietly. She grasped the sparkling violet cover and listened to the cigales as they buzzed and clicked in the night-time air.

Several days and nights had passed since the party in the pine trees. Most of the Snuffle-Buzzers had begun to think that Charlie had made the whole story up about discovering the violet book and having his glittering powers unleashed. So far, they had seen no evidence of the book, not even one fragment of glitter. The Snuffle-Buzzers buzzed amongst themselves. Charlie heard their muttering buzzes and he became very worried.

'Grand-cigale, I promise I didn't make it up just so you would let me go travelling. I really have found the book and I do have my glittering powers!' said Charlie. His grand-cigale nodded his head and buzzed in tune with his friends.

'The Snuffle-Buzzers do not believe me. Oh, Sevi, pleasezzz bring the book tomorrow,' Charlie said.

CHAPTER 9

BON VOYAGE

A hazy mist drifted along the valley and stacked low and solid in front of the holiday house on the morning the family were due to return home.

Sevi grabbed her backpack and headed into the forest where she gathered fresh sap from the pine trees and a small sprig of thyme leaves. She knew Charlie's glittering powers were working, but she didn't want to take any chances. Sevi placed the sap into a discarded cap from an empty tube of toothpaste. Smiling, she lodged the toothpaste cap into one of the swollen pockets of the orange wash sponge. She added two sprigs of thyme to another pocket and placed the sponge inside her backpack. Looking up, she felt the ghost-like, drizzly mist hover around her.

'Oh, Sevi, where are you?' said Charlie. He sat by the pillbox and watched as a cloak of steam rose from the forest floor and skimmed the branches of the pine trees. Charlie hoped that Sevi had not left without him. He blinked his big bug eyes and flapped his wings. 'Pleasezzz hurry and bring the book with you. They think I've made the discovery up!' said Charlie aloud.

Charlie's worries grew. Not only did Charlie worry about the book, but he had also started to worry that he and Sevi had not hatched a plan on how they would return him to the forest before late summer.

'Think it's this way to the pillbox, or is it that way?' said Sevi, with tiny beads of water springing from her hair.

Forest friends, Olivier and Gisele, watched from a weed-infested mound of earth as Sevi's dad loaded the camper van with luggage. Gisele reminded Olivier that it was not goodbye to Charlie but *au revoir*. The kitchen doorway looked as though a crack had formed in the plasterwork, but it was Stephanie, the stick insect, providing herself with a good view. Hervé's family of wild boars remained in the pillbox, but Hervé sat opposite the house under a cluster of late-blooming wild orchids and thought of Charlie.

With a buzz and a click, Charlie anxiously tapped his wings onto the stone pillbox. 'Oh, Sevi, pleasezzz do not leave without me, and more importantly do not forget to bring the violet book to the forest,' Charlie said, repeatedly.

The camper van bulged under the load. Canoes were in their travel boxes on the roof rack, whilst inside foldaway bicycles squeezed in beside the collapsible-hinged table. There seemed barely room for any other item, let alone Sevi and her parents.

Charlie sat as patiently as he could by the old winegrower's den of creativity. He had reduced his wing tapping to five taps at a time instead of ten. Still there was no sign of Sevi or the book.

The mist, now thicker, clung to the branches of the forest pines.

Worried, Charlie nibbled his front right wing. 'Where are you, Sevi? Are you lost?' said Charlie.

Once more, a group of Snuffle-Buzzers slurped their early-morning tree sap, buzzing as they looked over their wings at Charlie.

With the house keys placed underneath a potted yucca plant, Sevi's parents called for her as they stepped up into the camper van. Her name echoed across the valley and she heard the tail end of it, from within the forest.

'Vi, vi,' said the echo.

The mist swirled in front of Sevi as she jogged along the limestone trail. Sevi tripped over a raised tree root, and loose silk cobwebs whipped across her reddening face. She scrambled to her feet and ran, as quickly as she dared in the mist, hopping over pinecones and black millipedes.

A white cloak of mist circled her face. She heard the neigh of a horse and felt the wing of a butterfly as it swooped in front of her. The trees waved their branches briefly, applauding Sevi as she ran faster and faster through the white, chalky trail. 'How much further?' Sevi said aloud. 'Where am I?'

'Sevi, Sevi. Where are you?' called Charlie.

'Here, I think I'm here,' she said, as she dropped, out of breath, onto the ground in front of the stone pillbox.

'I thought I'd never make it,' said Sevi, gasping for air. 'I must have taken the wrong trail. I couldn't see a thing in this mist.'

'Oh, Sevi, am I pleaszzzed to seezzz you! Have you brought the book? Where is the book? I need the book! The other Snuffle-Buzzers have been buzzing about me all night and over breakfast sap this morning. They really do not believe me because I haven't sneezed glitter in front of them. They think I have made the whole thing up. The Snuffle-Buzzers are so desperate for their glittering powers to become unleashed,' said a very flustered Charlie.

'OK, settle down. Don't worry. It's here somewhere,' replied Sevi, grabbing a bottle of water from her backpack and taking a huge gulp. 'Good job this isn't a library book or my dad would have had one huge fine to pay,' Sevi said, pulling the mystical violet book from her backpack and taking another gulp of water.

After fastening her hair back into a ponytail Sevi scrabbled on the forest floor, dislodging a few creepy crawlies as she cleared a space for the book. Within a minute she placed it with its sparkling cover into a shallow hole and sprinkled twigs of thyme and pinecones all around it.

Charlie shook his wings with happiness when he saw his grand-cigale land on the pillbox.

As the mist cleared a little, a flash of violet, purple and gold glitter spun in the air above the shallow hole.

'Will the other Snuffle-Buzzers find it?' asked Sevi to Charlie.

A loud constant buzzing filled the air above them. Sevi looked up to see a huddle of flickering wings amongst colourful sparks of glitter.

'I think they just have,' replied Charlie, watching as each Snuffle-Buzzer in turn swooped onto the book's cover. Their noses of raspberry red and apple green shone brilliantly.

Set upon set of lattice wings hugged Charlie, Master Cigale. The young Snuffle-Buzzer that Charlie had spoken to at the pine tree party was the last cigale to show his gratitude; he did so with an enormous sneeze of golden glitter! Charlie's grand-cigale buzzed and buzzed with delight.

Sevi picked Charlie up and placed him in an empty pocket of her wash sponge.

'Yippeezz, off we go,' said Charlie. 'Oh, do you know the way?'

'It's left from here. I know where I am now,' said Sevi, as she hurried along the limestone trail back to the top of the vineyard, where she passed Hervé. A stitch pained her side as she ran across the meadow, over the dusty dirt track and up the steep gravel drive to the holiday house.

Through the rising mist, Sevi's dad spotted her as she ran towards the camper van. Just as Sevi opened the sliding side door and climbed in, her dad started the engine. Sevi's mum sat beside her dad and keyed their destination into the satnav. The two-toned beige and apricot vehicle drove along the gravel towards the dirt track. A shower of white powder from the gravel chippings sprinkled a family of ants as they once again scaled the terrace in search of leftover breakfast crumbs.

Sunlight glimmered and the ghostly mist danced above the mountainside.

Two water-bombers on a fire-practice-flight thundered overhead drumming out the sound of the camper van as it rolled along the track.

Corinne flew from the Roman chapel to bid farewell to Charlie. She was much happier with his travel plans. 'I say, Charlie, have fun, have fun, I say,' cuckooed Corinne.

Charlie clicked and buzzed just once in response to her call. The rumble from the camper van's engine and the water-bombers roaring overhead disguised Charlie's buzz. Charlie retreated further inside the wash sponge and dreamt of a distant land.

Sap swished inside the toothpaste cap so Charlie slurped as much of it as possible. His little belly rolled over in excitement. 'I've actually gone further than the streamzzz and row of plane trees! Yippeezz!' said Charlie, softly, but loud enough for Sevi to hear.

The family retraced their journey home. Tired and after many hours on the road, they stopped again at a northern French town. In the main square they found a shop which sold chocolate, bread and fancy cakes. Sevi took Charlie out of her backpack and this time he took his place looking out of the top pocket of her denim jacket. Both Sevi and Charlie enjoyed gazing through the window where they saw sweet frosted jellies and cakes in white fluted cases. Curls of white chocolate decorated the tops of orange cream sponges that were glazed with a smooth, dark chocolate icing.

'Wow! They look yumsville, but I had better get you back inside the wash sponge before Mum and

Dad come out of the shop with the baguettes,' said Sevi. Charlie nodded in agreement.

Once back in England and many driving hours later, the camper van pulled off the main road and entered a country park. There the family enjoyed a picnic. They ate red and white radishes, crunchy cornichons and crackers, poppy-seed baguettes filled with blue veined cheese followed by sweet, rosy-skinned apples. From their thermos flasks they drank peach-flavoured iced tea.

Charlie had drunk all of the sap from the toothpaste cap so he decided to go exploring.

Cows and sheep milled about the fields and the hedgerows bustled with tiny bugs. Close to a rabbit's warren, a shrub patch filled with nettles made an ideal eatery for hairy caterpillars. Sparrows and song thrush flew high and low.

Sevi's parents rested on a hillock amongst daisies and golden buttercups. Wasps droned and honeybees bopped upon the daisies. Peppered amongst the blades of green grass was a family of tiny red ants; they looked like red full stops.

Sevi placed some uneaten baguette inside her backpack then stood to stretch her legs. She was unaware that Charlie had ventured out of the wash sponge and had chosen to feast further on fresh dock sap. Although Charlie did not usually drink dock sap, he was thrilled with his find. He jigged about and accidently landed on a stinging nettle; the prickly hairs soon made him return to the dock leaf.

'Buzzing bananas! That's a stinger and a half,' said Charlie.

Sevi was about to take another sip of iced tea when she saw Charlie wiggling on the dock leaf, trying to remove the sting from his belly.

Sweat clung to Sevi's hands and her tongue stuck to her teeth. She took a sip of iced tea, but most spurted from her open mouth onto her jacket. 'Stay where you are, Charlie. If you move Dad will spot you, and it might trigger him to ask me which book I actually did take on holiday!' whispered Sevi.

'Bizzy, buzzy, sneezy lemon squeezy,' sang Charlie.

'Umm, look away, Dad, look away from the dock leaves,' muttered Sevi under her breath.

Charlie continued gorging on sap, singing softly and daydreaming under a parade of puffy white clouds.

'Stop stressing it. With any luck he might have forgotten about the violet book. It was donkey's years ago when he found it and kept the book from Henny,' said Sevi quietly. She hurried to the camper van to fetch a cloth to mop up the iced tea. 'He must have forgotten all about it,' she said.

On the other hand, had he?

'Buzz, buzz.'

Just as Sevi heard a buzzy-click, a hot air balloon with a group of six people hovered above them. The pilot fired the burner of the balloon and heat rose up inside its centre.

'Ooh, this is more like it! Warmth, heat, ummmm,' said Charlie, as he flew towards the wicker basket beneath the big red balloon. His wings grabbed one of the leather bands that cradled the basket and he whooped with joy!

Sevi had one eye on Charlie as he dangled from the basket, and the other on her parents as they carried the picnic blanket back to the camper van, before taking their rubbish to a waste bin.

'Charlie, what are you doing up there?' asked Sevi.

The red, bulbous balloon made its ascent into the sky, looking like a swollen plum tomato. It soared higher and higher.

'I'm not a wobbling gollywhopper this time. Whoo hoo!' buzzed Charlie. He gripped onto the leather band of the wicker basket, lapping up the warmth from the burner. 'Buzzzzz, buzzzzz.'

Charlie became more daring, and as he lifted part of his body off the leather band the warm air tickled his belly. 'Yippeezz!'

Charlie was unaware of how high the balloon had taken him until he looked right and left, then up and down. 'What am I doing? I'm far higher than I have ever been before,' cried Charlie. 'Oh no, I'm starting to feel a bit dizzyyyyyyyy!'

Charlie had lost his concentration and grip. Round and round, he twirled. Out of control and tumbling at great speed, Charlie flapped his wings wildly. Unable to balance his flight, Charlie plunged further and his lattice wings bashed against his body. 'Argh!' cried Charlie.

Sevi ran back to the camper van and grabbed the wash sponge from her backpack. She thought it would make a comfortable landing stage for Charlie, so she placed it on the grass near to the dock leaves.

Charlie tumbled further, but just before hitting

the tops of the giant oak trees he sneezed. 'Achoo!' Charlie's sneeze of glitter drifted through the treetops wrapping sparkling coils around him. With a crackle, violet and gold sparks popped sideways from the golden parcel. Charlie's glittering powers guided him safely towards Sevi's orange wash sponge.

The cigale had landed!

'Whoa,' said Sevi, as she scooped up the sponge with Charlie's bug eyes peering out of the golden parcel of glitter. Glittering sparks zoomed into the air, leaving only a trace of glitter upon Charlie.

'That was a hot flight, but you have to admit a super-cool landing!' said Charlie, wiping violet glitter from his belly and staring hard at Sevi.

Sevi carried Charlie back to the camper and placed him inside the backpack, with seconds to spare, before her parents returned from their visit to the waste bin.

Charlie slept soundly. He only woke when the camper van drove over the Tamar Bridge into Cornwall, and he felt a tickling sensation in his nose.

CHAPTER 10

KERNOW "ONE AND ALL"

The cottage where Sevi lived with her parents was in the heart of a small Cornish fishing village. Sevi's dad had lived all of his life within the thick, stone walls of the cottage, firstly with his parents and then with Sevi and her mum. (By the time Sevi's grandparents had decided to follow their lifelong dream – to live on a riverboat – her dad was earning enough money to buy the cottage from them.)

The stone cottage sat tucked behind the village church at the end of a narrow twisty lane which was barely wide enough to fit a car. Not far from the cottage was a coastal path which led to a steep set of wooden steps. At the bottom of the steps was a craggy cliff-hugging cove with teal-green waves and a soft, sandy beach. Blue mussels clung to the rocks and this is how it got its name – Blue Mussel Cove.

Sevi enjoyed her life in Cornwall. When the sun shone she ran across the moors and coastal paths, played football, climbed trees, swam and fished for mackerel and bream. Her ability to fish was first-rate, and she often caught larger fish than her best friend Jowan.

On dull, wet days, Sevi found nothing nicer than sitting in the conservatory with its twinkling lights. She read endless books, played hand-held computer games and sketched for hours on end.

Sevi's dad made her a climbing wall which she exercised on regularly. From the top foothold she nearly always managed to sneak-a-peek over the hedge into her neighbour's back garden. One day whilst she was watching her neighbour, Mr Lubber, as he gutted fish on his back lawn, he accidently cut his finger. He had called the fish pesky, slimy, fishes and wished he had thrown them to the grey seals whose thick, blubber bodies slumped on the slippery Cornish rocks.

On asking Mr Lubber if he was OK, the thought of oily-skinned fish had given Sevi a slip of the tongue. Whilst she imagined Mr Lubber's head attached to the body of a huge, furry grey seal, she had called him Mr Blubber instead!

~~~

Sevi looked through the window of the camper van and watched the sea mist drift over the bay. She heard a flock of seabirds and smelt the salty sea air.

As the white-wall tyres chugged along, Charlie stirred from his sleep and thought about the brilliance of his new glittering powers. With Charlie being allergy free, his throat no longer itched or felt scratchy. His sneezes of glitter only tickled his nose; they never made it feel sore.

'Achoo!' Suddenly a cascade of glitter fell from Charlie's raspberry red and apple green nose. The sparkling flakes circled the wash sponge before sinking into the orange pockets. 'Buzzing bananas! That's a surpriszzzingly large amount of glitter!' said Charlie. Amazed by the volume of glittering sparkles, Charlie checked his body and his wings; everything seemed to be in order. 'Umm, usually my glittering powers are most acceptabubble, but today I think they have gone bananas!'

Charlie's latest sneeze of glitter was far greater than he could cope with. Poor old Sneezlybuzzlebug!

'Out of control, it's really out of control. Too much glitter,' muttered Charlie, nibbling frantically at his front right wing.

The glitter occupied most of the orange pocket where Charlie stood. He waded wing-deep amongst the sparkling fragments. With his wings flexed and his head rolled back, Charlie braced himself as he battled against the glitter that filled the sponge with gem-like twinkles. 'A winged bug needs more room,' said Charlie. With one Master Cigale breathing movement, Charlie blew hard against the orange fibres creating a tunnel system.

Charlie's glittering powers had switched to turbo-twinkling and his agile wings struggled to keep up with the excess glitter. Through the open window shards of sparkling glitter vanished into the salty sea air, but much of the glitter remained within the sponge. Charlie continued to sweep the shiny fragments into the tunnels, dislodging some of the thyme leaves that Sevi had placed in the pockets. It seemed that the faster Charlie swept the more the sparkles rolled underneath his wings and laid flat against his sides.

After several minutes, a very tired Charlie stopped what he was doing and looked along the spongy corridors. His wings ached from all the pushing and sweeping. 'Buzzing bananas,' cried Charlie. 'Grand-cigale didn't tell me that Snuffle-Buzzers with glittering powers sneezed this much glitter. Why do I need so much of it?'

What would Charlie do with all the sparkling glitter, and why had his sneeze of glitter been so great?

Charlie had worked so silently on his tunnelling project that Sevi had not heard his fluttering wings or his gasping breath.

Fortunately for Sevi, her parents were unaware that a small live creature from Provence had accompanied them back to Cornish shores. Charlie was a souvenir with a difference; his home remained far away and he needed to return there by late summer to re-train for the Bugsect Multi-Buzz Championship. Charlie still had not a scrap of an idea of how he would manage this so, once more, he nibbled the curve of his front right wing.

The beige and apricot coloured camper van turned onto the steep, narrow driveway of the family's stone cottage. The sea mist lifted, a gentle breeze blew and the sun shone through the leaves of three Cornish palm trees, welcoming the family home.

Planted on the edge of the front lawn were pale-yellow primroses that flowered in the spring. They huddled next to large, deep-crimson rhododendron bushes. These were Sevi's favourite.

Sevi's dad picked up the mail from the doormat whilst her mum opened each one of the small leadlight windows in the cottage.

Floorboards creaked randomly under foot as Sevi carefully carried her backpack into her bedroom. Honeysuckle stencilled-walls were free from shadow. A golden glow lit the room and a pair of finely woven curtains, hanging over a small bay window, bellowed in and out from the breeze.

On the back lawn the familiar sight of a flock of gulls met Sevi's eyes as she peered through the flapping curtains. Sevi turned and pulled open the circular drawer handle from the pine chest nearest the window. With her backpack already half-unzipped, she picked up the wash sponge and lowered it inside the drawer. 'There you go, Charlie. This is your holiday home,' said Sevi.

After shifting the glitter into numerous tunnels, Charlie was so very tired. He could not keep his big bug eyes open, and so, after making a little more space for his wings, he snuggled back down inside the glitter-filled wash sponge and fell fast asleep.

Five herring gulls squawked loudly and intrudingly around the back garden. They were probably after fish scraps from Mr Lubber's early-morning fishing trip. A gull tossed a dried piece of white bloomer loaf onto the flat roofed surface of the Cornish stone garage. Another seabird snatched the bread and knocked it onto the lawn, where it fell upon blades of green grass and petals of three-leaf clovers.

Sea salt drifted in the air as Sevi helped her dad unload the luggage and put some laundry into the washing machine.

After Sevi's mum returned from the village shops, the family gathered in the conservatory. There they ate their lunch of crab salad, followed by home-grown strawberries and clotted cream, from the local dairy. The conservatory was the only place in the cottage not to have leadlight windows, but large, plain panels of glass with French-style doors that opened out on to the back garden.

Outside, a potting shed, vegetable plot and herb garden lay to the far right of a small astro-turfed area with white metal football posts either end. Smoky-pink magnolia decorated the sides of an arbour which was near to a fishpond and was home to pond skaters and koi carp. At the rear of the garden, Sevi's climbing wall backed onto her dad's workshop where he carried out woodturning.

Following lunch, Sevi scrubbed the crusted mud from her walking boots and then headed for the garden. After twenty minutes exercise on her climbing wall, and no sightings of Mr Lubber, she ran indoors to see Charlie. Opening the drawer she saw that the cigale had his wings propped to the outer curve of his holey-home and was surveying his new surroundings.

'Thank you, Sevi, this will do very nicely. I also want to thank you again for returning the violet book to us Snuffle-Buzzers, and for helping me spread my wings further than the streamzzz at home,' buzzed Charlie. He had decided there was plenty of time to worry about such things as turbo-powered glittering sneezes, and how he would eventually travel back to his pine forest.

'You are welcome! Where has this glitter come from?' asked Sevi, as she looked at the sparkling tunnels.

'I only sneezed once! You know a regular sneezezzz. No scratchy or itchy throat, but then wham!' replied Charlie.

'A regular sneeze for an allergy-prone cigale with glittering powers you mean?' said Sevi, half-giggling. 'That means a sneeze of glitter if I am not mistaken?'

'Ummm. Adventurezzz are calling,' Charlie buzzed, ignoring Sevi as she pointed to the orange wash sponge which at that moment had a fountain of glitter popping out of one of Charlie's newly made tunnels.

A large gull with a VERY loud squawk flew by the open window. Charlie leapt out of the wash sponge, landed on Sevi's bed and covered his ears with his lattice wings.

'Buzzing bananas! What a hullabaloo!'

CHAPTER 11

GIFFY

A colony of gulls relaxed on the banked grass of the cottage. One very large and very noisy gull returned frequently that afternoon. Sevi found some dried baguette at the bottom of her backpack and so hurled it onto the lawn. The bread skimmed the wafer-thin leaves of a peony, and a couple of pale-pink blooms drifted onto the grass.

The fragrant smell of a climbing rose wafted up into Sevi's bedroom. Charlie noticed that his glittering powers were firstly working well, and secondly working differently. Neither did his throat itch and nor did he sneeze glitter. 'Umm very interesting. No snuffle which is excellentzzz, yet no sneeze of glitter either,' said Charlie, as he jumped merrily upon Sevi's bed. The bouncy bedsprings sprung Charlie higher and higher so he had a fair view out of the window.

'That does not surprise me! You have sneezed stacks of glitter already today,' said Sevi.

'You don't think my glittering powers have become faulty after all that turbo-twinkling do you?' asked Charlie.

'Nope, I don't think so. The violet book controls your glittering powers. It's probably giving you a rest after the avalanche of glitter it sent your way earlier,' said Sevi, looking out of the window.

The gulls on the lawn interested Charlie greatly. It was on Charlie's highest jump that the largest of the seabirds had noticed him. The bird shook his head, most uncertain as to what he had seen, and went to take a closer look. The large gull with white and grey feathers stood motionless on the tiled ledge outside the window. Charlie also decided he wanted a better view and so speedily fluttered his wings towards the leadlight pane of glass.

The gull's beak opened and closed at regular intervals, snap, snap, snapping all the time.

'Am I the main course?' Charlie asked, as he glanced nervously at Sevi. The gull lifted a portion of bread and flicked it from his beak. The forcefully thrown bread bashed against the windowpane. Charlie rolled backwards with his belly sticking up into the air and his lattice wings shaking. 'What is it with me and windows? If I'm not being hurtled through one, I'm being attacked by a piece of bread near one,' said Charlie, trying to regain his confidence.

The gull's huge white wings flapped briskly and noisily against the pane of glass. Bug eyed, Charlie looked up at the gull. The gull's corn-coloured beak pecked at the window. His round eyes, with orangey-red rims and deep-black pupils, stared at Charlie. Scared that the bird with the large beak would eat him, Charlie jumped, clicked and buzzed all at the same time.

One further peony petal drifted to the ground, and a parliament of owls surveyed the goings on from an owl box attached to the garage wall. Silence reigned.

'I definitely think he is offering you the wings of friendship,' said Sevi.

'Are you sure? I suddenly feel nervouszzz,' buzzed Charlie anxiously.

The glitter underneath Charlie's wings flashed a brilliant shade of violet.

A small voice spoke. 'Hello.' It was Charlie's voice, but he, himself, hardly recognised it.

Sevi watched closely, as Charlie rocked from side to side. Wings flapped, eyes bulged, and cheeks flushed red then… a frightful noise filled the air.

'Raahhh ahhhh ahhhh ahhhhhhhooo.'

'That thing really has to stop doing that,' whispered Charlie, as the gull, whose cry sounded like a witch cackling in the wind, stepped from the tiles to the windowsill.

'Are you OK, Charlie? You'll get used to them. They can be a little greedy for food scraps, but mostly they are harmless.' As Sevi spoke, the very large gull winked, and through the half-open window lowered his neck towards Charlie.

'I can't understand him, but I think he definitely wants to make friends with you!' said Sevi to Charlie.

Sevi held Charlie in her right palm and the gull squawked repeatedly. Charlie winced at the noise and then the gull offered him his left wing. The seabird nodded his head gently and encouraged Charlie to climb onto his feathers.

'Go on, go on, Charlie. He really does want to make friends,' encouraged Sevi.

'Hop on, bug. I'm Giffy the Gull, "Head Gull" actually, on the account of me being the largest and wisest gull in this bay.'

Charlie beamed. Sevi was right. Giffy had lowered his wing to Charlie as an offering of friendship.

'OK, OK, this could work. With those massive wings I'll be able to travel in luxury over the waves and high up into the cliffszzz,' buzzed Charlie.

Giffy's soft feathers tickled Charlie's own wings and together they squawked and buzzed.

'A bit quieter on the squawking pleasezzz, if you don't mind,' said Charlie.

'I'll do my best, but I can't promise anything. Young critters of today,' said Giffy, as he raised his wings and squawked some more.

'I didn't mean to be impolite. If you can put up with my buzzing and clicking, I'm sure I can get used to your squawks,' replied Charlie, with a smile.

Charlie looked up at Giffy and thought that he seemed like a well-meaning gull and one that his forest friends would approve of. 'I think I've made another new friend!' Charlie said, quietly. 'This travelling business makes me super-happy!'

The flock of gulls that had been on the lawn earlier that afternoon had flown to the fishing harbour. In their place male and female blackbirds prodded the lawn in search for worms. With leftover breadcrumbs on offer, the blackbirds hastily pecked each remaining crumb until there was none left.

Giffy flew fast up onto the flat roof of the garage, but Charlie had not quite nestled into Giffy's feathers and so somersaulted into the air. Not used to having a travelling companion, Giffy soared over the fishpond without noticing that Charlie had fallen.

'Waitzzz!' called Charlie.

Charlie buzzed around the garden chasing after the wide-winged gull. 'Buzz, buzz!'

'Wiggle, jiggle those wings, Charlie!' shouted Sevi, forgetting that her parents were in the conservatory with the window open.

Eventually, Giffy held his wing out for Charlie to re-join him. The gull and the cigale gracefully ascended into the sky. Charlie nodded to Sevi and she smiled back.

Giffy coasted along the country lanes and over the slate roofs until he reached a small fishing harbour with many anchored boats. In a dash, Giffy had lowered his body and swooped up a vinegar-flavoured chip from the quay. Charlie gulped! The chip was only a little larger than he was, and so Charlie hoped Giffy would not mistake him for a tasty seaside snack.

Fishing nets and lobster pots decked the quayside. The abundance of small vessels in the harbour confirmed there would be food for Giffy, and plenty of it, but that could wait.

'Charlie, would you like some food?' asked Giffy.

'Yes pleasezzz, but I can't eat the sort of things you eat,' replied Charlie, looking worried.

Giffy's beak opened to a smile. 'Am I guessing right if I say sap?'

'Screaming seabirds! Spot on, Giffy.'

With Charlie clinging to Giffy's left wing, they flew over the headland to a thicket where Charlie slurped vast amounts of fresh sap.

It was later that evening before the sun had set when Charlie and Giffy returned to the harbour. Lights from the harbour-side cottages gleamed over the water where the gull and the cigale danced over fishing boats and lobster pots. Giffy's eyes glowed as he feasted happily on fish heads and discarded shrimp tails. Charlie, full from slurping tree sap, nestled under one of Giffy's wings and snoozed under the setting sun.

On the headland, a greedy gull looked on with envy in his eyes!

CHAPTER 12

COAST, CLIFFS AND CRUMB MATS

It did not take long for Charlie to settle into Cornish life. His friendships with Sevi and Giffy grew each day. Giffy proved to be a trusty and loyal friend to Charlie. Their jaunts took them over slated rooftops of whitewashed buildings and stone cottages. They flew beside the craggy coastline where ripcurl waves crashed upon sandy beaches, and paragliders soared above the cliff tops like giant prehistoric birds. Charlie, being the daring little cigale that he was, often stood on Giffy's wing feathers whenever Giffy glided over the water.

Sevi and Charlie visited the local fishing harbours and beaches. Sevi carried Charlie in the meshed section of her backpack where his views were always excellent. Sevi often took Charlie high up on the cliffs kite flying, then afterwards they beachcombed the shores below. Charlie was always keen to point out anything shiny on the golden sand.

On warm, sunny days, Charlie swam in the rock pools and sunbathed on the seaweed.

Often Sevi would sit on a grassy knoll with Charlie

perched on her shoulder. They'd watch as fishing vessels tacked their way into the small inner harbour of the busy port. At the tip of the outer harbour, a lighthouse stood guard above the jagged rocks.

Each morning before Sevi and Charlie left the cottage, Sevi scrambled up her climbing wall with Charlie as a regular companion. Sometimes, however, Charlie sneaked off to the eaves of the workshop where he played with the spiders and explored amongst the beams and rafters.

Sevi scaled the purpose-built climbing wall with ease. Charlie nearly always followed Sevi's climbing route; he flew from one foothold to another, except when he felt lazy, and then he just hitched a lift on Sevi's safety helmet and didn't bother to fly at all.

At the base of the climbing wall was a rubber crumb mat, which Charlie liked very much. Sometimes, instead of flying from the top foothold to the ground, he somersaulted – on purpose – landing each time on the mat with a buzz, a bop and a bounce!

Charlie had made new friends to share the summer with and he had a new place to sleep, albeit a glitter-filled wash sponge inside a pine chest. Charlie had no clue why he needed so much glitter; he guessed the violet book had ideas of its own.

CHAPTER 13

BED AND BREAKFAST

When the twinkling conservatory lights switched to sleep mode, Charlie settled down within the wash sponge inside Sevi's pine chest. Tucked up warmly within the glitter-filled tunnels, Charlie slept soundly.

The drawer of the pine chest, where Charlie slept, had a large gaping hole in the panel of wood. Before Sevi set up Charlie's holiday home there, she frequently lost pairs of socks through it. However, this hole suddenly proved useful because it allowed fresh air to flow into the drawer.

When the owls left their owl box to go hunting, the glitter shifted silently within the tiny orange tunnels, adding more to Charlie's supply beneath his sleeping wings.

With the early-morning chirping of blackbirds, Charlie yawned then slurped some fresh sap from the toothpaste cap.

With an aching front right wing, Charlie wiped his face. He then folded his wings gently over his back, sprinkling some glitter onto the bottom of the drawer. 'Umm, it's very interesting. I have woken again to an even fuller supply of glitter underneath my wings, yet the sponge is still packed with the stuff. It's amazzzzing that I can still fly. There must be a reason why I need all this glitter,' Charlie mumbled, sweeping the sprinkles of glitter into the corner of the drawer.

A long way away in Charlie's forest, where tall pine trees grew above a valley of goblet grapevines, the mystical violet book with its spine of purple letters sparkled once more.

CHAPTER 14

A CIGALE, RAGWORMS AND A SEA-MONSTER

Whilst sitting on a grassy knoll, Sevi and Charlie gazed over the bay and awaited the arrival of Jowan, Sevi's school friend. Jowan had recently attended a surf-school workshop; he was a keen and dedicated young surfer. Although skilled in the use of his soft, single-finned board, he and Sevi often used his bodyboard at Blue Mussel Cove.

Sevi opened her backpack in search of her favourite clotted cream sweets, but to her disappointment all she saw was a box of fish bait! 'Oh well, no sweets! I wonder if we will go fishing with Jowan's dad,' said Sevi aloud, looking down at the punctured air holes she had made in the lid.

Before Jowan arrived, layers of light and dark-grey clouds billowed and puffed in the sky. A large cloud resembling a flying horse joined to form an even larger one, similar in shape to an oversized ball gown. Both clouds rolled united over the West Country sky, splashing tiny droplets of rain upon Sevi's forehead. Charlie hastily climbed back inside the meshed section of her backpack and listened to Sevi's instructions.

'Stay there, Charlie. It's best that Jowan doesn't see you, or he may tell my dad,' whispered Sevi, glancing over the bay at the teal-coloured waters where mackerel bathed in silence.

'OK, I'm OK. I'll stay here,' replied Charlie, eagerly peering out of the mesh to see buoys bobbing on the surface of the sea.

After a few minutes the raindrops ceased, and a small glimmer of sunlight shone from behind the flying horse and ball gown.

Jowan jogged over worm-cast grasses towards Sevi. With his bodyboard underneath his right arm, he nodded his head and quickened his pace.

Charlie decided a little peek outside of the meshed section would not do any harm. He was small and agile; no one would see him. 'Umm, where to now?' wondered Charlie. He looked over to Sevi with his bug eyes and wrapped his wings around his belly as if to hide behind them. Had she seen him? He didn't think so. Where would he go? He needed to hurry, after all he had promised to stay within the mesh.

'Hi, Sev, how was France?' asked Jowan, as Sevi fetched a pair of sunglasses from her backpack.

'Buzzing! How was surf-school?' replied Sevi.

'Great thanks. There were three others all about my age. All stronger swimmers than me, so I'm gonna have to swim every day to improve,' said Jowan.

'Screaming seabirds! Jowan's heading for the backpack!' exclaimed Charlie. Jowan laid his bodyboard down on top of the long-stemmed grass, but accidentally knocked the backpack onto its side, which left Charlie dangling helplessly.

Charlie straightened his wings and then crawled up the outside of the blue, nylon material. He thought he was out of Sevi and Jowan's line of sight when suddenly…

'What was that?' asked Jowan.

'What was what?' said Sevi, hopeful that Jowan had not seen Charlie.

With an idea brewing, Charlie jumped. He intended to escape Jowan's stare. Charlie thought he could scramble away and still have time to go on a five-minute exploration, but his plan failed. Charlie's front right wing hooked onto a small, rough piece of nylon material. He was stuck, trapped and as still as a statue. 'Oh no, help meezzz,' said a flushed-face Charlie.

Charlie pulled gently this way and that way, but he could not move.

'It looked like a winged bug, but one I haven't seen before. Hey, you didn't bring anything back from France in that backpack of yours did you?' Jowan asked, as he chuckled and bent down, wanting to take a closer look at Charlie.

'Only these almond sweets for you,' said Sevi, quickly unzipping a side pocket and handing Jowan a narrow box. 'You're lucky I didn't open them earlier. I was peckish.'

'Why do I have to keep nibbling my wing? I've made the edge uneven,' Charlie said aloud.

The more Charlie tried to free his wing from the nylon, the more entangled it became. Sweat poured from Charlie's face, dripping onto his raspberry red and apple green nose, before bouncing onto his wings.

Distracted by the almond sweets, Jowan turned his head away from Charlie and sat on the grassy knoll next to Sevi.

Suddenly, glitter blasted from beneath Charlie's tangled wing and spun around the nylon material. Within a short time his wing was no longer tangled and the golden glitter vanished into the air. 'My under-wing glitter stores are becoming very useful indeed,' said Charlie. 'Thank you, glittering powers!'

Faster than one of Charlie's buzzy-clicks, the little cigale shook his wings and quickly crept towards the carry handle. Unfortunately, just as Charlie approached the handle, he tripped head-over-wing, dropping belly-first into the backpack. 'Whoaaaaa!' cried Charlie, as he fell. He raised his head and lifted his wings. 'Ouch! Help meezzz!'

Charlie's glittering powers struck again! A flurry of diamond-bright sparkles burst from beneath Charlie's wings. Firstly, the glitter swirled around Charlie, which soothed his aches and pains. Shortly afterwards, the glittering powers sent streams of shimmering, golden glitter out of the bag towards the teal-coloured waters of the bay. Deep-green waves rolled onto the shore, dragging small specks of golden sand and more of Charlie's sparkling glitter out to sea.

Charlie watched as the whirling glitter burst out of the open backpack with a fizz and a pop into the Cornish sea air.

Jowan opened the packaging of the narrow box,

offered a sweet to Sevi and returned his attention to the backpack. 'Oh, it's gone. Too much sun and surf. I'm seeing things,' said Jowan.

Charlie crawled around inside Sevi's backpack. 'What's thiszzz? It's hot in here and a bit smelly,' buzzed Charlie, as he stood on top of the bait box.

Charlie wanted to investigate further, so he sneaked through a medium-sized air hole in the lid of the box. There he played an exceptional game of hopscotch as he jumped over newspaper wrappings filled with ragworm. When Charlie's game finished, he rolled about letting the ragworms mingle over his bug eyes, his wings and on the top of his belly. The more Charlie rolled, the more newspaper print transferred to his wings. 'Whooo!' called Charlie.

'Did you bring any fish bait?' Jowan asked Sevi.

Before Jowan had given Sevi a chance to answer, he was already rummaging inside the backpack. He pulled the bait box out and squinted through the air holes. Charlie slid from one side of the bait box to the other. Under a sea of tumbling ragworm, he struggled to catch any air. Charlie kept perfectly still as Jowan opened the lid to the box and peered inside.

'Great, ragworm! I was thinking, if you don't mind let's go to the harbour and grab an ice cream. We can then head to the cove, so I can practice my swimming. The bait will keep for another day,' said Jowan, shaking the bait box full of ragworms and one allergy-prone cigale with glittering powers.

'Phew, that was a closezzz one,' Charlie buzzed, as he once again bumbled about over the fish bait. Finally,

Charlie squeezed through an air hole, scuttled up the inner material of the backpack and stepped upon one of Sevi's hands. Sevi felt Charlie's wings flicker on her palm and remembered the day his glittering powers were unleashed.

'Yes, ice cream and cove, good idea. I just need to put this on. I'll catch you up,' replied Sevi, waving a tube of sunblock at Jowan.

Jowan picked up his bodyboard and headed in the direction of the bustling fishing harbour.

'Charlie, are you OK?' asked Sevi.

'Yes, I am now,' Charlie replied.

'Excellent,' said Sevi. She quickly placed Charlie back inside the meshed section and hurried after Jowan.

Sevi and Jowan sat on the quayside and ate soft-whipped Cornish ice cream drizzled with raspberry sauce.

'I'd really like a pasty from that shop over there, but better not as we are going swimming. Anyway, I prefer the ones your mum makes – tasty and traditional with just the right amount of salt and pepper,' said Jowan. 'I've never known her to make a bad pasty.'

'They're made to the same Cornish recipe as the ones in the shop!' said Sevi.

'Yeah, and they make me super-happy!' replied Jowan, with a smile.

'You just like EATING!' said Sevi, laughing.

Charlie listened to the children as they chatted away about this and that, pasties with pepper and swimming, and before Charlie heard another word he had fallen asleep.

Sevi and Jowan removed their shoes and raced each other over the mossy-grassed coastal path above Blue Mussel Cove. They ran until they believed their feet could carry them no more, collapsing with laughter on the grassland.

Emperor dragonflies, on a visit to the beach, jiggled their wings towards the glistening sea. Once again, Charlie ignored Sevi's instruction to stay within the mesh. He scrambled free from the backpack and joined the cluster of dragonflies.

Shredded pieces of dark green and rich black seaweed strewn over the beach presented an obstacle course for the children as they ran shoeless to the clear rock pools. Hundreds of blue mussels clustered on the rock face of their favourite cove, and honey-coloured sand with shards of golden glitter rippled repeatedly through their toes.

Whilst Sevi searched the beach for quartz, Jowan unpacked his bodyboard from its carry bag.

'I'll have a go on the bodyboard, before my swim,' said Jowan, looking over at Sevi.

'OK!' called Sevi. 'Don't go too close to the inlets.'

Charlie flitted around the cove enjoying his freedom as he wiggled his wings alongside those of the emperor dragonflies.

Within minutes of Jowan being out at sea, he appeared to be distressed. Fear struck.

Charlie stopped relay flying with the dragonflies and dashed towards the young surfer. Jowan splashed his arms fiercely against the waves. The dragonflies with their green and blue bodies speedily flew from the beach and crags back to their riverside home as a Portuguese man-of-war quivered a hair's breadth distance from Jowan.

'Buzz, buzz, buzz, I don't think this fellow wants to make friendszzz!' buzzed Charlie, loudly and continually over the top of Jowan's head. 'He means business.'

Jowan's face turned white with fear. His arms, covered in goosebumps, splashed hard against the rolling waves. He wanted to yell but couldn't. The Portuguese man-of-war grew closer and closer. Charlie buzzed louder and louder as the tentacles of the purple-blue sea-monster stretched towards Jowan.

Sevi dropped a lumpy quartz rock from her hands, when she heard Charlie's buzzing and clicking across the sandy cove.

'Watch out, Jowan, watch out!' shouted Sevi, as she ran towards the shoreline.

As Sevi sped across the blackened seaweed, a funnel of twinkling glitter fell from beneath Charlie's wings. The whirling sparkles forced Jowan's bodyboard up into the air. As a further cone of glitter burst from Charlie's wings, the bodyboard spun faster and faster, and then with one huge plop landed flat on top of Jowan's attacker.

The glitter rolled amongst the waves and covered the tentacles of the sea-monster which gave Jowan chance to escape.

Sevi reached for Jowan's hand and pulled him towards her.

It was over.

Exhausted, Charlie swiftly flew back to the safety

of the backpack. 'What a monster and a half!' said Charlie, shaking glitter from his wings.

Breathless, the children staggered back to the welcoming golden sands.

'Phew, Jowan, are you alright? I haven't heard any reports of them invading us this year,' said Sevi.

'Yeah, I'm alright, but crikey that was incredibly dangerous. We had better inform the coastguard,' said Jowan. 'Have you got your mum's mobile on you?'

'Yeah, I have, but I won't get a signal until I'm up on the coastal path. I'll head up there now and call home. Mum or Dad will report it for us,' replied Sevi.

After Jowan recovered, he walked over to the narrow pipe near to the entrance to the small cove. There he washed the salt from his bodyboard without noticing the fragments of glitter.

Sevi dialled her home phone number, and with one bar of battery life left she got through. Whilst Sevi waited for Jowan, she sat on a grassy knoll and spoke to Charlie. 'Thank you, Charlie, thank you so much. Jowan could have been badly stung. At first I heard your buzzing, and then when I looked I couldn't believe my eyes,' said Sevi. She wanted to wrap her arms around the brave and fearless cigale, but he was far too small.

'My glittering powers came to the rescue again. I didn't do much,' said a bashful Charlie.

'Oh, I think you did, Charlie, and for showing such bravery you will have an extra supply of sap as a treat. Just imagine if you had stayed in the backpack. Next time I say to stay inside, just ignore me!' replied a very proud Sevi.

'Hah! I knew the glittering powers were giving me more glitter for a reason. The extra glitter helped to keep Jowan safe today. Thank goodnesszzz for that very large sneeze of glitter I did in the camper van,' said Charlie, as he looked out across the bay where a light sparkle rolled over the waves.

As the children walked along the coastal path towards Sevi's stone cottage, Jowan was convinced that the loud buzzing he had heard above his head came from one of the dragonflies. Charlie smiled.

A flickering of glitter sprinkled through the mesh, landing on a leaf of a silver spear plant, as Sevi opened the gate into her front garden. Once inside the cottage, Sevi went straight to her bedroom and squeezed Charlie in amongst the glitter-filled corridors of the orange wash sponge. There he slurped sap from the toothpaste cap and thought how marvellous his glittering powers were.

Downstairs, Jowan keenly told Sevi's parents of his earlier calamity. Sevi's dad told them that after Sevi's call, he had alerted the coastguard and Jowan's father to the afternoon's events. After listening to Jowan's news, Sevi's mum prepared afternoon tea.

Still taken aback by the whole incident, Jowan shook his head and followed Sevi into the conservatory. Within no time, Sevi and Jowan were gazing at a large selection of cakes and sweet, white bread rolls with home-produced strawberry jam and clotted cream. Whilst they sat eating a slice of cake and planned their next excursion, a whirlpool of glitter chased the sea-monster far from Blue Mussel Cove.

CHAPTER 15

ICE CREAM ATTACK

Morning arrived accompanied with the haunting shriek of gulls as they flew over the cove. The waves rolled back and forth upon the sand and the blue mussels looked polished after the night tides had washed their surfaces.

Sevi dressed into shorts and a T-shirt and then carefully placed Charlie inside the meshed section of her backpack. After breakfast she set off to meet Jowan at the harbour master's office. There she saw Jowan with his uncle. Sevi guessed he was probably telling him about the recent sea-monster incident.

It was a clear day with a gentle breeze as fishing boats docked in the harbour. The fish trade had begun. The smell of freshly caught bass, conger eel and bream travelled the length of the quay. Greedy gulls dipped their wings and snapped their beaks as they flew above the trawlers that were full with wriggling fish.

'Please stay in the backpack. Don't go sightseeing on your own and I promise I'll take you to the headland later. You can explore as much as you like there,' pleaded Sevi.

'OK, I know the drill, but if I had stayed in the backpack the day that purple and blue sea-monszzzter paid us a visit, what would have happened then, huh?' buzzed Charlie, defensively.

'Fair point, but please, just for a little while, stay where you are,' replied Sevi.

'I am just saying! Anyway, you said not to listen to you the next time you told me to stay inside the backpack,' said Charlie, cheekily.

'I know I did, and you are right. Jowan could have been seriously stung without you and your glittering powers. I'll tell you what, after we've been to the headland I'll take you to the aquarium. I think you'll really like the seahorses.'

'Excellentzzz!' replied Charlie.

The sweet smell of soft-whipped vanilla ice cream tempted Sevi to check in her pockets for coins. A few minutes later Sevi clutched her newly bought ice cream and strolled over to the local gift shop, where she took a seat on a wooden bench next to the doorway.

Sevi stared out beyond the harbour walls to the vast, gaping, teal-green sea. Small, colourful fishing boats bobbed up and down, and the gentle sound of waves lapping against the tide marked walls of the inner harbour almost sent her to sleep.

The sun glistened on the windows of the white painted lighthouse. Gulls screeched their laughter high above the cliffs and village of slate roof cottages. Rising and falling in the breeze, they flapped their strong wings and raced around the harbour in search of their next free dinner.

'Coucou, I'm still here,' called Charlie, as he looked through the mesh at Sevi.

'Hello, my little mate! Bet you can't wait to go to the aquarium?' asked Sevi. However, before Charlie had time to reply...

'Raaahhhhhh ahhhhha ahhhhhhooo!' cried the greedy seabirds.

Sevi had taken her eyes off her ice cream for too long! Three gulls swooped at her feet jumping and squawking, eager to feast on the ice cream cone. Charlie peered through the mesh. He watched Sevi as she tried to eat the ice cream as quickly as she could. Within seconds more seabirds arrived, and they too greedily begged for some of Sevi's treat.

Sevi glanced at her backpack which was on the bench beside her. She watched her little friend as he strolled up and down behind the mesh nibbling his front right wing.

'Don't nibble it, Charlie, it will become very sore,' said Sevi. Charlie looked at her and nodded in agreement.

The smell of freshly caught fish hovered in the salty sea air, but still the greedy birds were committed to Sevi's ice cream cone. Some of the soft-whipped ice cream had melted and plunged to the ground, along with a soggy piece of cone. Beaks scraped and gnashed together as the gulls battled for the cone-shaped wafer.

Charlie continued to peek through the mesh; his eyes widened as he saw Sevi surrounded by ten greedy white and grey winged seabirds. Sevi ate faster and faster and yet it was not fast enough.

'Screaming seabirds! I wish they'd cool it a bit,' said Charlie. 'Where are their manners?'

The quayside uproar caused Sevi to accidently knock her backpack onto the ground. Charlie's little body jolted forward onto the hard, concrete quayside. A fearless gull knocked the remainder of the ice cream cone out of Sevi's hand as she leant forward to pick up Charlie and her backpack.

Plop! Charlie's bug eyes were level with the blob of white ice cream that had dropped onto the quay. He took a few dazed steps and walked straight into the hollow bottom half of the cone. The fearless, greedy gull opened his beak wide, snap, snap, snapping. He lowered his head and speedily scooped up the cone, with Charlie inside, and made for the lighthouse.

'Help meezzz!' buzzed Charlie, but the waves carried his cry and the seabirds laughed.

The sun stretched its rays over the lighthouse, fighting a bank of fuzzy white cloud from the west. Charlie wiggled inside the mouth of the greedy gull as it tottered up and down on the metal slats of the lighthouse deck.

Sevi stamped one foot on the quay and clamped her right hand over her mouth. Her chocolate-brown eyes gazed fearfully towards the tall, white lighthouse. 'No! Whatever will become of Charlie?' choked Sevi.

Sevi squinted and strained her eyes against the summer sun as she tried to catch a glimpse of Charlie.

In the distance the fuzzy white cloud had rolled by, but there was something casting its shadow over the lighthouse.

Nervously Sevi tapped her hand onto the side of her legs when she suddenly had a thought. 'Money, that's what I need,' she said, pulling her last coin from the side pocket of her shorts.

Sevi ran across the quay to the seaside telescope where she placed the money into the slot, angled the telescope towards the lighthouse and watched eagerly as the shadow over the lighthouse grew bigger. It was the widespread wings of Giffy as he swept over the teal-green waves, casting his shadow over the white sides of the lighthouse. With his beak pointed like an arrowhead, he lunged and pecked fiercely at Charlie's captor, but still the greedy gull would not set Charlie free.

Trapped and scared, Charlie let out a muffled cry. 'Help meezzz!'

Once more, Charlie nibbled his front right wing.

The cigale pushed and pushed against the soggy cone, aiming to flee from the gull's snapping beak. However, the beak of the gull snapped shut just as quickly as it had opened. Charlie pushed forward, but his aching front right wing dragged behind, making it impossible for him to escape. What could he do?

Charlie heard the waves as they crashed against the lighthouse, but he could not see them.

Sevi's eyes became tired from staring through the telescope at Giffy. She rubbed her fingers over her long lashes and then once again gazed through the telescope, watching Giffy hop from one metal slat to another.

Although Charlie's front right wing still ached, he

managed to adjust his wings whilst inside the mouth of the greedy gull.

The beaks of the two gulls bashed and crashed together, but more than two pairs of wings flapped!

Swirling around behind the snapping beak, Charlie flapped his wings, giving the gull the full force of his glittering powers.

A magnificent jet of gem-like twinkles burst from beneath Charlie's wings. Similar to a hosepipe spurting water, the jet of glitter swished around the inside of the gull's mouth.

'Ahhhhraaahhhhggghhhh!' choked the greedy gull, as he coughed and spluttered.

On the deck of the lighthouse, amongst sparks of glitter, were the remains of a very soggy ice cream cone and, of course, Charlie.

Covered from head to wings in glitter, Charlie's glittering powers sent another jet of gem-like twinkles up towards his captor. 'Plpuff, splurrr, plpuff,' spluttered the gull, as he skidded about all over the deck.

'Raaaahhhhhhhhhahhhahhhhhhhhhha,' squawked Giffy, as he stood beak to beak with Charlie's captor on the glitter-sprayed metal slats.

'Go, just go!' ordered Giffy to the greedy gull.

Another shower of glitter swirled around Charlie, removing every piece of soggy ice cream cone from his lattice wings.

A gigantic swell of seawater rose so high it hit the deck of the lighthouse, rinsing it clear of sparkles and forcing the smaller gull to admit defeat. At last, squawking loudly, he flew from the tall, white lighthouse and perched on a rocky mount.

Salty seawater splashed against the rocky mount, drenching the greedy gull and removing the last trace of glitter from behind his snapping beak.

With a final, envious glance at Charlie and Giffy, the gull flew with soaked wings hard and fast over the crashing waves, chasing the shadow of another fuzzy white cloud.

'Am I glad to seezzz you,' said a glittered-out Charlie.

'I don't think you needed my help at all, my little bug!' replied Giffy, as he offered a wing to Charlie.

'Well, I suppose my glittering powers helped quite a bit.'

Sevi had seen most of the action through the old seaside telescope. She stood on the quayside, smiling, as Charlie clung to Giffy's left wing.

'You'll have to tell me about these glittering powers of yours, but before I return you to Sevi do you fancy a bit of Giffy-gliding?' asked Giffy.

'Think I'll give it a misszzz if you don't mind. I've had quite enough excitement for one day,' buzzed Charlie.

The shrieking calls of seabirds bounced off the rugged cliffs that were dotted with pink thrift. With each shriek, Charlie nuzzled further amongst Giffy's wing feathers, shielding their screeching cries.

'Heh, you two! Thanks, Giffy, but I must say, Charlie, your glittering powers are fantastico!' said Sevi. She tucked Charlie inside the mesh and waved at Jowan as he made his way along the quay with two melting ice creams!

'Oh no, ice creams. I hope I don't seezzz that greedy gull again!' said Charlie, once more nibbling his front right wing and looking eagerly through the mesh.

CHAPTER 16

RARE BAT V RARE CIGALE

After a visit to the aquarium, Sevi returned Charlie to the glitter-filled corridors of the orange wash sponge and then went to watch a television programme.

Within minutes of Sevi leaving the room, Charlie flew out from the broken panel in the chest of drawers, through the open bedroom window and headed towards the sea. Charlie had been to Blue Mussel Cove many times with Sevi, so he knew the way.

When Charlie reached the cove he landed on a clump of blackened seaweed next to a rock pool of clear water.

The orange sun slowly snuck out of sight, hiding below the horizon. Soon afterwards, the moon's glaring white face provided Charlie with a clear view of Blue Mussel Cove. There on the sand, Charlie spotted something glinting under the moonlight. 'I must tell Sevi. She loves quartzzzz,' said Charlie, looking closely at the precious rock.

The waves lapped onto the shore and Charlie thought how peaceful it was. It was not until he heard a high-pitched sound, causing him to cover his ears with his wings, that he thought differently. 'Heh! Keep it down! I'm trying to get some me time,' said Charlie to a flying mammal that flittered around the night-time sky.

Moonlight continued to shine above the craggy cliffs and sandy cove. Charlie stared dreamily into the rock pool, but before he had chance to think many thoughts the mammal making the high-pitched noise once again flittered above his head. With a shake of his wings he rose into the air and chased the sound across Blue Mussel Cove. 'I say, if you don't mind can you be a little quieter?'

Charlie perched on one of the rocks that jutted out into the sea. The moon gave enough light so Charlie saw that Blue Mussel Cove was more than a sandy beach; it was home to a family of bats.

Charlie flew around the craggy cliffside watching as a tiny plum-sized bat disappeared along a narrow inlet. Chasing the bat's high-pitched shout, Charlie fluttered his wings and he too flew above the teal-green waters of the inlet.

Within no time, Charlie had reached the entrance to a cave. Before venturing further, he called out. 'Helloooooooo! Are you in there? Some of my friendszzz at home are batty, I mean are batszzz,' said Charlie. 'I'm sorry if I upset you, but when you flew near to me your shouts were too piercing for my ears!'

Charlie took a deep breath and headed inside the cave.

'Well, if that's your attitude you can buzz off. No bat invited you here,' said a voice that came from high up inside the rough-roofed cave.

'Charming! You are not as friendly as the bats at home,' replied Charlie.

'I'll have you know we are rare lesser horseshoe bats and we need our privacy. This is our winter home,' said the tiny plum-sized bat, as she dangled from the cave's roof.

'I'm rare too, a rare breed cigale,' said Charlie. 'Hang on, a winter home, but it is summer. You've got more than one home?' asked Charlie.

'I am hanging on, and yes, we have a summer one too, or at least we did have. Anyway, it's none of your buzzziness!' said the bat, suddenly remembering to be rude.

'Summer, winter, makes no differencezzz to me,' said Charlie, as he turned to fly out of the cave.

Charlie heard the sound of dripping water, and upon looking up he saw the plum-sized bat dangling from the roof of the cave, sobbing her heart out.

'Well, I'll be off then,' said Charlie, suddenly feeling awkward.

'Wait. Please. It's just that we have lost everything. The humans came in and cleared the place. A barn conversion, that's what they called it,' said the weeping bat.

'A barn conversion, what's one of those?' asked Charlie.

'It's a barn which is turned into a house for humans. Before the conversion the barn was our summer home,' replied the bat, as she started to cry again.

'Well look, stop crying and I will seezzz what I can do,' said Charlie.

'Do? What can *you* do?' replied the bat, getting rather upset.

'OK, if you are going to be like that I'll say goodnight and leave you to your bat cave. Unlesszzz you would like to join me outside for a moonlight flight?' said Charlie, with a soft voice and wide-open eyes.

'I really should eat you, but I'm not into foreign food,' replied the bat.

'Really, you are impossible,' said Charlie. 'Some bats just don't know when they are well off.' He flew out of the cave and returned to the rock pool. There he sat quietly and thought of the seahorses which he had seen at the aquarium.

Before long he heard the high-pitched shout from the bat.

'Sorry, I truly am,' said the bat. 'Can you really help me?'

'I think I might be able to, but first, what's your name?' asked Charlie.

'Bat,' said the bat. 'Just Bat.'

'OK, Just Bat. Give me a tour of your bat cave and then I'll take you to your new summer home. After all, you and I have something in common, we are both rare,' replied Charlie.

With that, Charlie and Bat flew over the sandy shore, along the inlet, back to the deep, dark cave.

The moon shone through the opening to the bat cave. Charlie followed Bat inside her cold, dark winter home. As Charlie dodged a large granite boulder, he thought that he much preferred his forest, but not wishing to upset Bat further he kept quiet. Bat flew mega fast around the cave wondering what type of summer home Charlie had in mind; she too thought it was best to keep her thoughts to herself.

Water dripped from the walls of the cave, and before long Charlie decided he had seen enough and that it was time to leave.

With a fluttering of wings, Charlie screamed as two bats flew towards him at great speed. 'Argh!'

'Stop! Don't eat him. He is my friend,' said Bat to her two older brother bats. They did not listen and gripped Charlie, pinning him to the green, mossy cave wall.

'I said STOP!' cried Bat, but her brothers still had a firm grip on Charlie.

Charlie tried to flutter his wings, but before he had a chance the brother bats shouted their high-pitched call, which caused Charlie to shudder from the noise.

'Argh, it hurtszzz my ears!' cried Charlie, once more.

The rolling waves sparkled under the moonlight, rippling onto the sandy beach.

Whilst inside the cave, a flurry of glitter swirled out from beneath Charlie's wings, finally freeing him from Bat's older brothers. The two bat brothers looked at each other in amazement, then shook gold and purple shards of glitter from their little plum-sized bodies.

'Listen here, you two, we need help, and Charlie says he can help us find a new summer home. He is a rare breed cigale and understands how important it is for rare creatures to live as comfortably and as safely as possible. You know we should only live here in the winter. We can't afford to keep giving our supply of insects to the greater horseshoe bats as rent all year round.'

Charlie's glitter whirled, like one of the dirt track dust devils, around the floor of the cave.

Nodding in agreement with their younger sister, Bat's brothers returned to the roof of the cave, where they hung upside down trying to catch their breath.

'Right then, are you ready?' asked Charlie, adjusting his wings. Charlie smelt the salty sea air and flew towards the mouth of the cave. Bat followed, thoroughly embarrassed by her brothers' behaviour.

Charlie flew across Blue Mussel Cove with Bat flying beside him.

'Can't you fly any faster?' asked Bat.

'Don't start. I'm going as fast as I can,' said Charlie.

'Sorry,' said Bat. She kept quiet for the rest of their flight.

'Ta-dah! This is your new summer home,' said Charlie, as they approached the woodturning workshop.

'Well, it's not exactly a barn is it?' said Bat.

'Noooo, but it is a suitable home for the summer. You have a family of owls over there in the box attached to the garage. The roof of the workshop is big. I've explored in there myself a few times,' said Charlie.

Bat flew to the eaves of the workshop and tried her new summer home out for size.

'Oh, Charlie, actually this is rather nice,' said Bat quite softly.

'Good. Oh and, Just Bat, did you meanzzz it when you said I am your friend?' asked Charlie, blushing.

'Might have done,' said Bat with a half-smile, as she dangled upside down in her new summer home.

CHAPTER 17

DREAMS AND SPARKLING WISHES

Bat and her brothers had settled into the eaves of the workshop. They were very happy with their new summer home.

Most evenings when Charlie returned to the wash sponge after visiting Bat, he thought of snapping beaks and fountains of sparkling glitter. It had been several weeks since the ice cream incident at the lighthouse, but Charlie could not stop thinking about it. Each time Charlie thought about the greedy gull, or any other thing that troubled him, he nibbled his front right wing. 'I have to admit, I'm flying more and more like a wobbling gollywhopper each day,' said Charlie aloud. 'I really must stop nibbling or I will never fly properly again.'

One starlit night whilst Charlie slept inside Sevi's wash sponge, his glittering powers once more set to work. The enchanted glitter shifted within the orange tunnels and rolled underneath Charlie's lattice wings, dislodging not only the toothpaste cap but the sap as well. Within a short time, the glittering sparkles streamed out of the broken panel and through an open fanlight window. The glitter drifted into the cool night-time air towards the dark bay with its fast-rolling waves.

Charlie dreamt of many things that night. Behind his closed bug-eyelids, Charlie recognised the violet book, which the old winegrower had sealed with mystical charms of rich glittering powers. The glittering powers were his friend; they not only helped with his allergies, but also came to his aid in times of need. His dreaming eyes saw his pine forest under a shower of golden, violet and purple glitter. Charlie folded his front right wing over his raspberry red and apple green nose and snoozed some more. He dreamt of his grand-cigale, and watched as he hovered above the violet book with its spine of purple letters. Each letter danced and sparkled beneath the branches of the tall pine trees. Each pine called Charlie's name, and the gold-edged pages of the violet book rustled beneath a canopy of glitter.

The cackling laughter of a flock of seabirds woke Charlie the next morning.

A new supply of glitter lay neatly underneath each one of Charlie's wings. Traces of glittering sparkles clung to the orange tunnels, but for the most part the glitter appeared to have vanished. 'What now, glittering powers? Where's my glitter?' Charlie asked, as he tiptoed out from the wash sponge.

Charlie looked around the shadowy drawer which felt safe, but lonely. He leant forward, and then with a leap darted through the broken panel of wood.

Charlie flew lopsidedly towards the windowsill.

102

Looking out of the leadlight windows, he spotted Sevi on her climbing wall. She had started her exercise without him. Charlie lowered his head and wondered why.

Sweeping a wing over a diamond-shaped section of glass, Charlie cleared a patch of condensation. Looking downwards, he noticed that two peony leaves had a sprinkling of violet and purple glitter upon them. However, it was not long before a drizzly rain shower trickled down the slate rooftop of the Cornish stone cottage and rinsed the glitter from the peony's leaves.

Charlie sat making wishes and each wish came with a flurry of glittering sparkles and a glow of violet wings.

After many minutes, Charlie thought of his grand-cigale…

'Oh, my grand-cigale, whatever should I do?
I keep dreaming of glitter and wake to seezzz it too.
The sparkles sprinkle on my wings and help in
times of need,
My allergies have all cleared up; I am snuffle free.
I dreamt last night of forest pines. I stirred during my sleep,
I saw the purple letters sparkle. I felt the pinecones creak,
I gather the time is nearing for when we soon shall meet.
My pine forest is calling me; I feel it week by week,
The glittering powers of the violet book will forever
be unique.
My wings hold still the glitter that twinkles constantly,
I guess I'll have to shake the mix and flap my wings
times three.

*The charms within the violet book, I hope will then
guide me.
The glitter that flows amongst the deep, dark sea,
Will forever watch over young, carefree Sevi.'*

Still staring out of the window, Charlie watched as
Sevi stepped down from her climbing wall and ran
indoors.

Sevi climbed the twisty staircase to her bedroom
and saw Charlie with his eyes shut, clinging to the
bottom window frame. Sevi reached forward, picked
Charlie up, and carried him to the pine chest of
drawers.

'Umm, there's hardly any glitter in the wash
sponge!' Sevi said, softly. Believing that Charlie was
asleep, she gently placed him inside one of the orange
pockets. 'Oh, and the toothpaste cap is empty, the sap
has gone. I can only see traces of glitter in the wash
sponge. How strange!'

Charlie kept his eyes tightly closed.

'See you later, sleepy head! I reckon you've been
having too many late nights with Just Bat! Anyway, you
could do with a rest; soon you will have a long journey
ahead of you! I'll come back for you this afternoon and
I'll take you to a thicket, where you can have as much
sap as you want,' whispered Sevi, looking down to see a
trail of glitter on the base of the drawer.

'Bye,' choked Charlie, so quietly that Sevi never
heard him, as she closed the wooden drawer and left
the room.

CHAPTER 18

THE SNUFFLE BOX OF OGGIES

Sevi grabbed her fishing gear from the garage and checked the date on her watch. Summer was ending; she could feel it in the early-morning mists and light drizzly rain. Tourists were fewer and although she still sat on the grassy knolls, overlooking the bay, it was not so warm.

Late summer only meant one thing: Charlie was to return to his forest and start re-training for the Bugsect Multi-Buzz Championship. Sevi knew life without Charlie would be very different.

With a sigh, Sevi jogged from the garage to the front of the stone cottage. She crossed the lawn, glanced at the rhododendron bushes, and then hurried along the twisty lane that led to the busy fishing harbour. All the while she thought of Charlie. How would he travel home?

Sevi met Jowan and his dad outside the harbour-side gift shop. Then, with patchy light-grey clouds rolling by, all three walked along the quay to Jowan's dad's fishing boat. Cackling gulls swooped over the small boat as it bobbed up and down on the teal-green waters.

Weak, late summer sunshine briefly shone onto the glass of the white lighthouse and the swell from the sea splashed against its walls. Giffy circled the lighthouse several times. As he glided through the air, he too wondered what route Charlie would take to travel home. With an idea brewing, he flew to Blue Mussel Cove and thought it through.

Wide awake, Charlie tiptoed out of the orange wash sponge. He flew once more to the windowsill, but this time he climbed through the open window. With a flitter and a flutter of glittery wings, he was gone.

In the kitchen of the stone cottage, Sevi's mum had just completed the third and final batch of Cornish pasty baking. The kitchen units were full of traditional pasties (or oggies as the villagers called them). Warm beef, onion, potato, swede, salt and pepper lay silently within the golden-glazed pastries.

Everyone in the village said how delicious the pasties were. However, due to a slight technical hitch, these three batches would taste a little more peppery! Sevi's mum had just added the salt and pepper to her mixing bowl when she had heard the phone ringing. By the time she reached the phone, the caller had rung off. She returned to her kitchen and washed her hands, but just as she lifted her mixing bowl she heard the phone again! After taking the overseas call she hurried back to the kitchen. Completely forgetting that she had already added the salt and pepper to the bowl, she sprinkled another dose of each to the main pasty ingredients.

Charlie had flown from Sevi's window to the grass where he hovered above the tiny petals of three-leaf clovers. His bug eyes suddenly widened. 'Not again!' said Charlie, looking at seven large seagulls, all with eager eyes glaring directly at him. 'I am finding this most unacceptabubble,' said a frightened Charlie.

Panic-stricken, Charlie speedily, but lopsidedly, flew back to the cottage and crawled up the stone wall. The little cigale looked down onto the lawn, and then with a flutter and a jump he found himself inside the conservatory. The rows of twinkling fairy lights that decorated the windows dazzled Charlie's eyes, making him blink.

Safe from the seven large gulls, Charlie began to feel a little happier and so went exploring. On the glass table were three boxes of pasty parcels, almost ready for posting. 'Ummm, whatever the smell is, it's coming from these boxeszzz,' said Charlie, as he approached the table with fluttering wings.

The bottom two pasty parcels were sealed and ready for posting. The lid on the third was still open. The smell from the open pasty box grabbed Charlie's attention, so he flew towards it. Suddenly Charlie had a fuzzy feeling in his nose and his throat started to itch. 'Achoo!' Sadly, Charlie's sneeze was not a sneeze of glitter, but an allergy-prone sneeze. 'What? Why? Where are my glittering powers?' asked Charlie, glancing down to his front right wing which had started to ache.

'Achooooooooooo!' sneezed Charlie, once more. 'I think it's that pepper stuff Jowan spoke about that's making me sneeze!' Charlie's raspberry red and apple green nose became very sore. 'Buzz, achoo, buzz, achoo!' Once again, Charlie sounded like a one-bug band.

With a fluttering of wings Charlie twirled and twisted in the air above the open box, before he finally drifted downwards landing in between rows of warm savoury pasties. 'Pepper, pepper, pasty, pepper! Too much pepper!' cried Charlie, as Sevi's mum closed the box with tape and added an address label to the top.

Inside the pasty parcel, Charlie tiptoed in between the pasties. Suddenly, he remembered Sevi's bait box full of ragworms. He began to chuckle nervously as he thought of the game of hopscotch he had played. He could not play hopscotch with the pasties; these crimped-edged pastries were far too big!

Charlie's nervous chuckling stopped. He ran lopsidedly from one side of the closed box to the other. Eventually he fell onto his belly, tired, worn out and confused as to why he had not sneezed glitter. 'Where are my glittering powers?' Charlie said aloud. His throat itched terribly and there was no sap to soothe the sharp, scratchy feeling.

Charlie had nibbled his front right wing so much that his glittering powers were failing. He needed a set of working, flightworthy, whole lattice wings. What would he do?

The small fishing boat tacked into harbour. Sevi along with Jowan and his dad had spent all morning out at sea and had caught enough fish for two family meals that evening. A light breeze whipped through Sevi's wavy hair as she and Jowan stepped off the boat onto the quay.

Next to an old fish cellar, an angler re-baited a stack of three lobster pots and tidied his nets.

Hungry and tired the children walked briskly around the boat-filled harbour, through the village and along the twisty lane that led to Sevi's home.

'It was good of your dad to take the fish home with him to fillet. I can pop round later to collect mine,' said Sevi, as she and Jowan walked through the front door to the stone cottage.

After a quick wash and brush up, Sevi and Jowan ate lunch in the conservatory. All the pasties were boxed and ready for posting, so the children each had bowls of homemade tomato soup and soft-seeded, crumbly bread.

'That was nice. Think I'll have a little doze by the French doors. You don't mind do you?' asked Jowan. 'Afterwards we can collect the fish you caught.'

'Uh, oh yeah. That's fine,' replied Sevi, thinking it would give her time to check on Charlie.

Jowan soon fell asleep; he dreamt he was back on his surfboard skimming the teal-green waves.

Thump, thump, flutter, flutter, snuffle, and sneeze.

Jowan was unaware of the fluttering, snuffling pasty parcel, but Sevi turned her head and could not believe what she heard. Inside the top box of pasties came the sound of wings fluttering and a cigale snuffling.

'Oh my days! Charlie, don't tell me you are in the pasty box! What are you doing in there and why have your allergies come back?' said Sevi, very, very quietly.

Thump, thump, flutter, flutter, snuffle, and sneeze.

'Mum, thanks for lunch. If these pasty parcels are ready for posting, I'll run them down to the post office for you whilst Jowan's asleep,' called Sevi, not waiting for a reply.

Sevi quickly grabbed her backpack from a wicker chair and a reel of sticky tape from the side unit. Balancing the three pasty boxes on her open arms, she carefully opened the front door to the stone cottage. The afternoon sun glinted through the Cornish palm trees as Sevi walked steadily down the steep, narrow driveway and onto the twisty lane.

It was when Sevi was far from the stone walls of the cottage that she cautiously opened the snuffling box of oggies. She looked down into the eyes of the cigale and remembered the day she had found him in her tatty old suitcase, dazed and embarrassed. Charlie's face looked much the same at that moment.

'Charlie, my little mate! Whatever has happened? How did you get in here, and why are your glittering powers not working?'

'I went exploring. Umm, I think it's because of my front right wing! I've been nibbling it for weekszzz now, and because of that I am not a whole, rare breed allergy-prone cigale. My wing nibbling has reduced my glittering powers. I really need help! Even the glitter from underneath my wings was not enough to help me today. I have to get out of here. Too much pepper!' said Charlie.

'OK, let's go to the headland and think this through, but first I need to post the other two pasty parcels. You haven't sneezed all over them have you?' asked Sevi, with a half-smile.

'Umm...' said Charlie, looking towards the ground with his big bug eyes.

'Errhhh, germs,' said Sevi, placing Charlie behind the mesh in her backpack.

'I'm joking – no germzzz. Those boxes were already sealed, but there may be lots of that pepper stuff in those too!' said Charlie.

'Reckon you could be right! When I tell Mum about her mistake with the pepper she won't be pleased with herself. She has very high standards. Mum usually makes sure her pasties are traditionally perfect. I'll tell her that I sneezed all the way to the post office, and then she won't hesitate to throw these away and make some more batches!' said Sevi.

'Phewzzz! Hope she believes you. Don't want to get you into trouble,' said Charlie.

'No chance of that, my little mate! Mum will be glad that she will be able to fix the problem.'

Upon reaching the harbour Charlie's bug eyes scanned the teal-green sea for gulls. Only when he saw a fishing trawler dock with fresh fish did he relax. With no ice cream cone to encourage the gulls closer to him, Charlie blinked, and with a sigh he looked out to sea.

Giffy was amongst the seabirds scrounging fish scraps. The screeching laughter of the gulls echoed around the busy fishing port and bounced of the white walls of the lighthouse.

111

Sevi walked quickly to the headland where sea carrot spread over the grassy cliff tops. Once there, Charlie flew very awkwardly from the meshed section to a thicket where he slurped on fresh sap, which soothed his itchy throat.

'Charlie, after I went on my climbing wall this morning I checked the date on my watch. Do you know what I am going to say next?' asked Sevi.

'Why you went on the climbing wall without me?' Charlie replied, whilst still slurping sap. He raised his aching front right wing and then looked out across the bay.

'No, actually I was going to say it is nearly time for you to return to your pine forest. Oh, and just so you know, that is why I climbed on my own this morning. I was trying to get used to you not being around,' said Sevi.

'Buzzing bananas!' shouted Charlie.

'OK, I thought you would take it badly,' said Sevi, jumping up from a dry clump of grass.

'No, look!' said Charlie, pointing out to sea. He flew crookedly to Sevi's backpack.

Bursting from the teal-green waves was a fountain of Charlie's sparkling glitter. It was the very same twinkling glitter which had popped from the orange wash sponge the night before, sprinkling purple and violet sparkles over the peony leaves on its way to the deep waters of the Cornish bay. These fresh new sparkles mingled with the glitter that had streamed out to sea many weeks before, the day the blue-tentacled sea-monster visited Blue Mussel Cove.

Charlie stood on top of Sevi's backpack with his wings opened wide. The small amount of glitter underneath Charlie's wings spiralled all over him, but with his glittering powers working at half-strength, Charlie needed a huge boost from the violet book.

Far away in Charlie's pine forest, where birdsong rang out and butterflies with yellow and green wings swooped amongst the wildflowers, the violet book jiggled and wiggled under a stack of pinecones. The spine of purple letters flashed and a beam of golden light shot through each page of sealed charms. The glittering powers of the violet book willed Charlie's glitter to rush over the fast-rolling waves towards him.

Charlie balanced on top of Sevi's backpack. With a fast beating heart he watched as a super-huge wave splashed high above the cliff face, sending a dazzling shower of gold, violet and purple glitter towards him.

Quickly, Sevi stepped backwards and watched eagerly as, once more, a sparkling, twinkling coat of glitter covered the small allergy-prone cigale.

The Cornish teal-green waves calmed, and far away in Charlie's pine forest the violet book stopped jiggling and wiggling. The old winegrower's mystical mix had been as powerful as ever in coming to Charlie's aid.

On the headland, Sevi could not believe her eyes. 'Whoo hoo! Buzzing bananas!' she said, echoing Charlie's enthusiasm.

As Charlie twirled around, admiring a brand new set of lattice wings, he felt a tickling sensation in his raspberry red and apple green nose. 'Achoo!' To Sevi's and Charlie's delight, it was a sneeze of glitter!

Gold, violet and purple sparkles nestled underneath Charlie's new wings and a shower of the same coloured glitter vanished into the salty sea air.

'Wow! I think it is safe to say your glittering powers are working properly again! What a smashing set of wings you have, Charlie! No more nibbling,' said Sevi.

'Umm, reckon I could get myself a girl-cigale with this set of wind-wingers,' replied Charlie, once more admiring his striking new wings.

'It's great that your glittering powers have returned to full strength and you have fantastic new wings. There is only one problem to solve. How are you going to get home?'

CHAPTER 19

LATE SUMMER

With Charlie in the meshed section of her backpack, Sevi marched up the steep, narrow driveway to the Cornish stone cottage. She walked through the side gate to the back garden and saw Jowan gazing at the koi carp in the fishpond.

'You've been gone ages! I've been awake for over an hour! Shall we go and collect your fish? Dad will have filleted them by now,' said Jowan.

'Sorry. Yeah I'll be five minutes,' replied Sevi, touching the shoulder straps of her backpack.

As Sevi approached the wooden doorway which led into her bedroom, she noticed a small, brown paper bag on her bed.

'What's this? A brand new wash sponge,' said Sevi, as she peered inside the bag.

Carefully, Sevi took Charlie out from the meshed section and placed him on her duvet. She then ran across the creaky floorboards to the chest of drawers and pulled the circular drawer handle towards her. Her heart thumped so hard she thought it would punch itself out of her skin.

Speedily, Charlie flew to look inside the open drawer, which had been his safe haven for many weeks. 'Where's the orange wash sponge, Sevi? Where is it?' asked Charlie, about to nibble one of his brand new wings.

'Don't nibble!'

'Where is it?'

'I don't know,' replied Sevi, scrabbling in her backpack for her hair band. She tied her wavy strands into a small ponytail and started to tap the top of the chest of drawers with her fingertips.

'It's really darkzzz in there, but no different from underground, I suppose,' said Charlie.

'Dad's repaired the hole. You know, the broken panel. It's been replaced and with no ventilation you can't sleep in there!' said Sevi.

'I think I understand how Just Bat felt, when she lost her summer home,' said Charlie. A drop of sweat poured from his face onto his thudding belly.

At the back of Mr Lubber's garden, woodpigeons chortled within the rich leaves of a Cornish oak. On hearing their call, Sevi turned and glanced out of the window. There, on the glossy white windowsill, stood Giffy with a fish scrap hanging from his beak.

'Charlie, I have to go with Jowan to his home to collect the fish I caught this morning. Go out with Giffy and when I get back I'll try to stretch the holes in this new wash sponge and…' All at once, Sevi stopped speaking and lowered her head.

Charlie paced up and down on top of the chest of drawers. Neither Charlie nor Sevi spoke for several minutes; both were deep in thought.

'Don't worry about stretching the holeszzz, Sevi. Especially as I can't sleepzzz in the drawer anymore. Pleasezzz don't worry about anything. As you said earlier, I think it is time for me to return to my pine forest,' said Charlie.

With a red, blotchy face and a wobbling lower lip, Sevi nodded in agreement. She hung her head out of the leadlight window, breathed in the cool, late afternoon air and placed Charlie onto Giffy's left wing.

Late summer had definitely arrived. Charlie would be back amongst his forest friends, just as he had promised, before the leaves turned bronze and red berries graced the hedgerows.

Giffy swallowed the fish scrap, looked through the window and watched as Sevi placed the new wash sponge in the drawer next to the empty toothpaste cap. With her head held low, Sevi left the room without looking back over her shoulder.

'Where to, Charlie?' Giffy asked.

'Home, Giffy. It is time for me to go home,' replied Charlie.

'Yes, I thought as much, and being Head Gull I have thought of a plan to set you on your way,' said Giffy.

'Thankszzz,' said Charlie.

Charlie's new lattice wings burrowed into Giffy's feathers. The seabird and the cigale circled the lawn of the Cornish cottage. The owls poked their heads out of their bird box and the pond fish splashed against three lily pads. Bat and her brothers peered bleary-eyed out of the eaves and gave Charlie one last high-pitched shout. Charlie buzzed goodbye as he and Giffy swooped over the church rooftop, chasing the wind along the narrow twisty lane to the coast.

Sevi and Jowan raced each other to Jowan's seaside bungalow. As Sevi ran, her chocolate-brown eyes spilled salty tears onto her cheeks. 'It really was time for Charlie to return home and I'm sure Giffy will help him,' muttered Sevi.

'What did you say?' asked Jowan.

'Nothing, just thinking aloud,' replied Sevi, as she hurried towards Jowan's home.

The coastal bungalow where Jowan lived with his dad stood at the end of a hilly cul-de-sac. The flat lawn opened out onto a small side drive with views over the bay.

Jowan had forgotten his key, so he rang the bell. Jowan's dad arrived at the front porch, allowing the smell of pan-fried fish to waft out of the bungalow. He handed Sevi a cool bag with her fish nicely filleted inside, then returned to his kitchen.

'Thank you!' she said, looking sideways towards the bay. 'I had better get back. Mum will want to cook these.'

'Are you OK?' asked Jowan. 'Shall I walk back with you?'

'Me? Oh yeah, I'm fine. I just have something in my eyes. I'll see you tomorrow. No need to walk me back, it isn't far! Thank your dad again.'

Sevi jogged across the lawn, along the path to the end of the cul-de-sac then onto the lane that led to the dairy and the post office. Then, instead of going home, she headed towards the harbour. Sevi's throat tightened, as the sound of gulls cackled over the bay. She ran very fast along the coastal path to the headland; she wanted to say farewell to Charlie.

The headland grasses were damp. Sevi glanced at the thicket where Charlie often slurped fresh sap. He had been on loan to her, the same as the violet book had been to her family. Charlie belonged to a different climate with tall pine trees, truffles and wildflowers. The wildflowers with their special dyes had helped to create a world of glittering powers for allergy-prone cigales; it was these powers which had given Sevi and Charlie the chance to become friends.

Sevi buried her head into her hands; she had already started to miss Charlie.

'Raahhh ahhhh ahhhh ahhhhhhhooo!' screeched Giffy, as he glided by the white walls of the lighthouse.

Sevi looked up to see Giffy soaring over the teal-green waves towards her. There on Giffy's widespread wings stood Charlie, as Giffy glided over the deep, dark waves of the bay.

'Buzzzzz! Sevi look at me!' buzzed Charlie, as he spotted Sevi on the headland.

'Wiggle those wings, Charlie!' called Sevi, smiling.

'I will and thank you so muchzzz!' cried Charlie.

'Remember you have your full glittering powers back and a good supply of glitter underneath your new wings,' Sevi shouted, over the wind that whipped through her ears.

'It's been excellentzzz!' called Charlie.

'Giffy will help you. I'm sure his plan will be better than any I could have thought of,' said Sevi, as her voice charged over the waves to Charlie.

Suddenly a fountain of glitter rose from the seabed and splashed against the cliff side.

Charlie flapped his wings three times. He had shaken the mix.

Charlie called out to Sevi and although the wind carried his words in the salty sea air, the glittering powers stole their meaning.

The deep waves of the teal-coloured waters were there to watch over young, carefree Sevi, but she could no longer understand anything the rare breed allergy-prone cigale said.

Giffy flew fast, so it was not long before he and Charlie were out of Sevi's line of sight.

Evening was drawing in. Sevi hurried home with a cool bag of fresh filleted fish in her hand, and a hollow feeling inside her belly.

In the stone cottage the conservatory lights twinkled brilliantly, glowing onto the glass door of the reading room. The bookshelves remained full, except for a narrow slot where the violet book had once stood.

Whilst Sevi and her parents ate their fish supper, they looked out towards the garden. Except for the sound of the church bell ringing on the hour, all was quiet inside and out of the Cornish stone cottage.

CHAPTER 20

HOMEWARD BOUND

Giffy squawked loudly as his wings dipped into the swell of the sea. The gull with the cigale tucked within his feathers flew over the crashing waves. They passed rocky coves where pirates of old had smuggled possessions from ships that were now wrecks beneath the sea.

That night they took shelter along the coast where rugged, red rocks jutted onto the shore.

At first light, they headed further and further east. Giffy flew hard and strong, but frequently stopped to rest in woodlands and country parks. Charlie welcomed the opportunity to drink sap and flutter his new lattice wings in the early-morning breeze.

Charlie gripped Giffy's feathers tightly as the gull flew across towns, cities and parks.

'Are we there yet?' asked Charlie, his breath battling against the wind. Giffy shook his head and glided high over motorway lanes, jam-packed with vehicles of all shapes and sizes.

Cars, nose-to-tail, greeted the two aviators, when eventually they reached their destination.

'Here we are, my bug,' said Giffy, as he landed on top of a telegraph pole.

'What is this place? Have I been here before? Where are we?' asked Charlie.

'Oh, Charlie, too many questions. It is like the Spanish Inquisition,' replied Giffy.

'The what?' asked Charlie.

'The Spanish…' Giffy started to say, when something caught his eyes. 'Talking of Spain, see that van over there?' asked Giffy, nodding his head towards a van which read: "ARBOLES ORNAMENTALES BARCELONA". Next to the signwriting was an artist's impression of the flag of Spain. Beneath this was the British counterpart: "ORNAMENTAL TREES KENT" and this had a national emblem too, the Union flag. Smaller letters and numbers provided an internet site and telephone details. Artwork, on the sides of the van, showed a collection of small trees within violet painted pots.

'Which one? Oh, I seezzz, the one with trees painted on the sides,' Charlie said. As he balanced on Giffy's wing, he strained his eyes to see over the queues of vehicles.

'Well, my bug, in answer to your questions, this is the Channel Tunnel. It is an undersea rail tunnel. The train will take passengers and their vehicles to France. I would have thought this is how you travelled to England with Sevi, but I suspect she had you hidden somewhere safe,' replied Giffy.

'Yes, apart from when we stopped, I stayed inside her backpack. What's the plan then, Giffy, old boy?' asked Charlie.

'Less of the old, if you don't mind! Well, I think if we time it right you could travel in the back of that tree van. The driver will set you on the right path home. The van should take you nearly as far as you need to go, but it will probably mean a short flight at the other end,' said Giffy.

'Oh, I seezzz. The problem is… at home, I have never flown further than the streamzzz and row of plane trees. I might get lost,' said Charlie.

'Lost? Think of what you have done since you left home! You won't get lost,' said Giffy, flapping his wings and dipping his beak. He was hungry.

'OK, I'll do it. I am Charlie, Master Cigale, with full glittering powers after all.'

'Just listen for the sound of the cigales and you will know when it is time to leave the van,' said Giffy.

'How do you know all of thiszzz?' asked Charlie.

'I came first in Gull-Geography at Seabird School,' replied Giffy.

'How will I get out?' asked Charlie. 'Buzzzzz, buzzzzz.' Charlie started to warm up and his buzzing rang through Giffy's ears.

'He is human. He will need what humans call comfort breaks and rest stops. However, it will be when he stops the van to check on the trees that you must keep very still and listen carefully. If you don't hear the cigales stay on the trees, but if you do hear them, fly like the wind,' said Giffy.

'What if I oversleep and end up in Spain?' asked Charlie.

'If you do, well, then you can start your Bugsect

Multi-Buzz Championship training early against the Spanish cicadas, and on "away" pine trees!' replied Giffy, with a gentle chuckle.

'Buzzing violet tree pots! The driver has opened the rear doors of the van and there are at least seven small trees in there!' said Charlie, excitedly.

'Yes, my bug, and trees mean sap! Are you ready? It's been "buzzing bananas" as you would say, Charlie, having you fly with me. Hold on, bug!' said Giffy, extending his left wing.

Giffy flew towards the van, but as he headed for the back of the vehicle the driver had already started to close the doors. Giffy's wing speed increased, but he was too late. The van's doors slammed shut and the gull and the cigale had no choice but to land with a skid on the van's roof.

'Argh!' cried Charlie.

Then, quicker than one of Charlie's buzzy-clicks, the driver returned to his cabin, started his engine and drove towards the train carriage. Suddenly the van stopped sharply, which caused Giffy to lose his footing. Charlie fell from Giffy's wing and, with a thump, landed sideways onto the van's metal roof.

'Ouch! My new lattice wings,' called Charlie in dismay.

The driver stepped from his cabin. He had forgotten to tie back a couple of the small potted trees and so re-opened the rear doors.

All of a sudden a spray of glitter burst from underneath Charlie's new wings and showered him in violet, purple and gold sparkles. Giffy's eyes gleamed brightly as a cluster of glitter raised Charlie from the metal roof. It twirled him around and around in the air before directing him through the open doors of the van. Coils of the tri-coloured sparkles carried Charlie and laid him on top of one of the small ornamental trees.

Giffy flew from the van's roof and looked on in amazement. 'You never did tell me much about your glittering powers, but I can see that they are working well!' cried Giffy. 'Oh, and stay away from ice cream cones and lighthouses!'

'Byezzz, Giffy and thank you!' buzzed Charlie, at the same time as the violet book jiggled and wiggled in its shallow hole within Charlie's pine tree forest.

CHAPTER 21

TELEPHONE CALLS AND PHOTOGRAPHS

Heavy dew clung to each blade of grass on the back lawn of the Cornish stone cottage.

Sevi woke late with sore, puffy eyes and was disinterested in going on her climbing wall. Instead, she thought she would call Jowan. Just as she was about to ask to use the phone, Sevi saw on the telephone table a printed photograph and a note with dates and details that confirmed a booking at the holiday house for the following year.

'Oh, Charlie,' Sevi whispered, picking up the photograph which her dad had taken on their holiday. Sevi recognised the yellow and black coat of an owlfly, and on a closer inspection a silhouette of a small cigale, clinging to a pine tree.

Sevi smiled widely and, with a wave of excitement, dashed up the twisty staircase to her bedroom. She ran across the creaky floorboards, pulled open the drawer to the chest and picked up the empty toothpaste cap with one hand and her new wash sponge with the other. Sevi laid them inside her recently repaired suitcase and then went downstairs to call Jowan.

Three tiny pieces of glitter flitted from the open drawer, through the bedroom door, down the twisty staircase, along the hallway and into the reading room. Faster than a shooting star the narrow gap on the fourth bookshelf, where the violet book had stood for many years, closed.

CHAPTER 22

REMEMBERING HENNY

Heavy rain lashed against the leadlight windows of the stone cottage. Lights twinkled inside the conservatory and the scent of apple kindling, burning gently, mixed in the air with the warm smell of freshly baked pasties.

Looking puzzled, Sevi's dad stared at the bookshelves in the reading room. He knew every one of the books in his collection, and although the shelves were full there was one missing. It was the very book he had found when he was a boy, the small book with the violet cover.

Sevi's dad turned his head away from the bookshelves and watched as the rain splattered against the leadlight window.

Sevi opened the glass door to the reading room and walked in. Gently, she placed the photograph of the owlfly and cigale on the centre of the fourth bookshelf.

'Oh, Dad, I meant to say ages ago, you know I borrowed one of your books, well, I actually left it in the forest when we were on holiday. It was a small book, just a few pages with a violet cover. Sorry,' Sevi said, with her fingers crossed behind her back. She hoped that he, himself, would remember taking the book from the forest many years before.

Sevi's dad smiled, nodding his head at her. It was a knowing sort of nod.

As Sevi's dad looked towards the garden, drops of water fell either side of the leadlight window. He had remembered the adventures he had shared, as a boy, with Henny – the first Snuffle-Buzzer with glittering powers. He regretted never returning the mystical book to the forest. All he had ever wanted to do was to understand the twinkling codes, symbols and advanced Cigale-language, but the old winegrower's mystical seal around the charms had made it impossible.

Sevi's mum entered the reading room. She placed two serviettes and a round wicker basket with hot Cornish pasties on the table next to the armchair. When she left Sevi's dad took one last knowing glance at his daughter, flicked three specks of glitter from the fourth bookshelf and helped himself to a pasty.

'It's in the mix, Dad, it's in the mix,' said Sevi, as she too took a pasty from the basket and headed out of the reading room.

CHAPTER 23

VINES AND PINES

The villagers within the French valley of grapevines and pine trees heard the grating shriek of a rook and the high-pitched squeak of a pair of buzzards as they flew above the tree-lined mountain.

A light wind carried the gentle, buzzing hum of cigales.

Under a stack of pinecones the violet book rustled its gold-edged pages.

The holiday house had been prepared for the arrival of new guests. The black and yellow blooms of late summer sunflowers filled a colourful, hand-painted vase. Fresh milk, cheese, ham, olives, fruits and yoghurts filled the shelves of the fridge. Outside, the terrace showed no trace of dirt track dust.

Stephanie, the stick insect, had consumed almost her body weight in oak leaves. She returned to the pillbox at dawn where Gisele, the grasshopper, and Olivier, the owlfly, greeted her. Hervé's family of wild boars, exhausted from foraging, slept soundly for much of the morning, but Hervé was restless.

Hervé's chunky, rough-haired body rolled over.

He lay in the pillbox and daydreamed about the time three huntsmen in bottle-green clothes ran to capture a younger boar. Charlie had buzzed non-stop over the huntsmen's heads. He had flicked his lively lattice wings over their ringing ears then, with a twist of his body, he tickled their noses. Distracted from their quest, the huntsmen angrily jumped on the spot and waved their rough-skinned hands over their heads.

Hervé's eyes twitched as his daydream continued. He remembered how swiftly Charlie had alerted him to the huntsmen. This had given Hervé time to trot back across the meadow under the protective cover of a row of almond trees, and direct the young boar to the safety of an underground burrow.

Hervé smiled as he recalled seeing the mud-splashed huntsmen lose their foothold and skid into a mud-coated water gulley. Their swift arrival into the milky-chocolate trench would not have been faster had they travelled by bobsled.

Mosquitoes, ravenous for food, had nibbled at the huntsmen's sun-stained arms as they had attempted to climb up the sides of the gulley. Squelch, splash! After several attempts to clamber free from the mud, they eventually made it onto the grassy meadow above. Their ears spurted a sloppy, brown gloop, and their fingernails had received a sludge manicure.

With swollen red mosquito bites on their arms and no boars in sight, the huntsmen had staggered to their off-road truck and had driven away, very displeased.

~ ~ ~

Hervé rose from the uneven floor of the pillbox and gazed up at the pitted roof. He remembered the tale Charlie had told him about the old winegrower and his mystical mix.

Forest branches swayed gently, but Provence promised another warm day. Later that morning the forest friends settled under the shady umbrella of the tall pine trees.

Inside the van carrying small ornamental trees, Charlie slurped sap. His bug eyes widened as he suddenly remembered that he had promised everyone that by late summer he would start re-training for the Bugsect Multi-Buzz Championship. He looked around the van and wondered if, when he returned to his forest, Gisele would take him to the Limestone Grasshopper Gym. There he could do extra training for the championship in the steam room and finally help Gisele with her breathing exercises. Charlie thought it was a super-good idea and so drank more sap!

As Charlie's mind wandered, the van driver indicated to turn off into a service station. The van's rear doors rattled as the driver drove over a pothole to a parking area. Charlie was having such a buzzing time he had almost forgotten Giffy's instructions.

Whoosh. Charlie fell from a low branch, dribbling sap onto his new lattice wings.

'Are we there yet? Oh, I think we have stopped!' Charlie said aloud.

The small cigale kept very still and very quiet.

Charlie heard the driver's door slam shut and

the vibrating sound of heavy footsteps as the driver walked to the back of the van. Within seconds, the driver opened the rear doors, enabling Charlie to hear an orchestra of cigales. 'Oh! French cigales or Spanish cicadas!' said Charlie.

Charlie tapped his lattice wings onto his belly. Was it too soon for him to leave the van?

The driver checked on the trees and with only a nanosecond left before he closed the dented, metal doors, a rush of violet, purple and gold glitter burst from beneath Charlie's wings. It streamed swiftly towards the tiny gap between the two closing metal doors. 'I think this is my stopzzz,' buzzed Charlie, excitedly. He speedily flicked his wings together and flew out of the van, chasing the stream of glitter as it headed towards the valley of vines and pines.

The sun-bleached meadow opposite the holiday house was as tired as the wild boars. In the valley beneath the cover of several tangled threads of bracken, a wasp eagerly dragged a rumpled, beige-legged spider from sight. Ants marched single file across the forest floor under the shaded canopy of trees, and a small dark-haired dog, resembling an aubergine on legs, scampered along the dusty dirt track.

Unaided by any type of wind, a stack of pinecones rolled over the forest trail near to the pillbox.

The book with its spine of purple letters jiggled and wiggled, whilst rare breed Snuffle-Buzzers buzzed and clicked happily above the violet cover.

When Hervé heard the bells from the Roman chapel ring out at noon, he joined his forest friends.

Birdsong spread like wildfire throughout the vineyard and dense forest. Dogs barked from their outside kennels, and near to the curved bridge a grey horse drank from the slow-flowing stream.

As the afternoon sun reached the valley, the summer Mistral paid a brief visit. It came in stifling gusts, but brought no ash-grey clouds this time. Warm, windy air shifted white, puffball clouds along the azure blue sky. Dust devils welled in pockets along the track, but broke instantly as they brushed against the tyres of a red tractor.

'Whooo! I can seezzz the streamzzz and the row of plane trees, the forest of pines and Sevi's holiday housezzz. I'm home!' buzzed Charlie, as the warm, gusty air swept him through the vineyard. 'Oh, Sevi, if only you knew how much I'm going to miss you. I think I might even miss your backpack too!' said Charlie, with a chuckle.

Grapes, ripe and ready for harvest, bunched amongst lush-green leaves. Charlie flew alongside some fruit flies as they darted amongst the rows of goblet vines.

The summer Mistral lifted Charlie up into the air and in the direction of his pine forest.

Above the violet book, coils of gold, violet and purple glitter gently fell from beneath the lattice wings of Charlie's fellow Snuffle-Buzzers. Charlie's grand-cigale led the way as each set of wings sprinkled more and more glitter over the violet cover. After Charlie's family and fellow Snuffle-Buzzers had decorated the book with gem-like sparkles, they flew to the tall pine trees.

Hervé, Gisele, Stephanie and Olivier rested in silence under the shade of the pines.

Without a sound Charlie landed behind a windswept branch on top of the pillbox. Whilst he sat watching his family and friends he thought of many things. Charlie was grateful to Sevi for returning the violet book to the forest and for having his glittering powers unleashed. He thought about his adventures and he was truly thankful for having had the opportunity to travel. However, whilst he watched his family and friends, Charlie realised that he was super-happy to be home again amongst the limestone pine trails and valley of vines.

A shaft of sunlight peeked through wind-swept leaves. With a buzz and a click, Charlie tiptoed from behind the branch and stood on the edge of the pillbox. His friends and family looked at one and other. Each turned their heads to face the golden sun and, to their delight, they saw before them Charlie, Master Cigale.

With a whooshing of wings and a sprinkling of glitter, Charlie's ma-cigale and grand-cigale left their pine tree and returned to the shallow hole where Sevi had placed the book weeks before. On the violet cover, their merry dancing made the pinecones jiggle and the spine of purple letters twinkle. The cigala, (pine tree party) to celebrate Charlie's return, had begun.

'I think they are pleasezzzed to seezzz me,' said Charlie. With a buzzy-click, Charlie flew towards his family and friends, where he joined in the fun of the cigala. With cigale chitter-chatter echoing through the pine trees Charlie glanced at his new wings, and as they flashed super-violet he once more remembered Sevi.

As Charlie slurped tree sap and thought of how the old winegrower, many years before, had created the mix, sprinkles of enchanted, tri-coloured glitter swirled around his wings. As the glitter drifted towards the pillbox, Charlie smiled. He said softly, 'Buzzing bananas! Just imagine if they allowed me to use my glittering powers at the Bugsect Multi-Buzz Championship!'